MARY DOWNING HAHN

Deep and Dark and Dangerous

A Ghost Story

Clarion Books
New York

Clarion Books
a Houghton Mifflin Company imprint
215 Park Avenue South, New York, NY 10003
Copyright © 2007 by Mary Downing Hahn

The text was set in 13.5-point Octavian.

www.clarionbooks.com

Printed in the U.S.A.

Library of Congress Cataloging-in-Publication Data

Hahn, Mary Downing.
Deep and dark and dangerous / by Mary Downing Hahn.
p. cm.
Summary: When thirteen-year-old Ali goes to spend the summer with her
aunt and cousin at the family's vacation home, she stumbles upon a secret
that her mother and aunt have been hiding for over thirty years.
ISBN-13: 978-0-618-66545-7
ISBN-10: 0-618-66545-5
[1. Secrets—Fiction. 2. Ghosts—Fiction. 3. Mother and daughters—
Fiction. 4. Cousins—Fiction.]   I. Title.
PZ7.H1256Dee 2007
[Fic]—dc22
2006025652

MP 10 9 8 7 6 5 4 3 2

To everyone who enjoys ghost stories

One rainy Sunday in March, I opened a box of books Mom had brought home from Grandmother's house. Although Grandmother had been dead for five years, no one had unpacked any of the boxes. They'd been sitting in the attic collecting dust, their contents a mystery.

Hoping to find something to read, I started pulling out books—*Charlie and the Chocolate Factory, Misty of Chincoteague,* and at least a dozen Nancy Drew mysteries. At thirteen, I'd long since outgrown Carolyn Keene's plots, but I opened one at random, *The Bungalow Mystery,* and began flipping the pages, laughing at the corny descriptions: "Nancy, blue eyed, and with reddish glints in her blonde hair," "Helen Corning, dark-haired and petite." The two girls were in a small motorboat on a lake, a storm was coming, and soon they were in big trouble. Just as I was actually getting interested in the plot, I turned a page and found a real-life mystery: a torn photograph.

In faded shades of yellow and green, Mom's older sister, Dulcie, grinned into the camera, her teeth big in her narrow face, her hair a tangled mop of tawny curls. Next to her, Mom looked off to the side, her long straight hair drawn back in a ponytail, eyes downcast, unsmiling, clearly unhappy. Dulcie was about eleven, I guessed, and Mom nine or ten. Behind the girls was water—a lake, I assumed.

Pressed against Dulcie's other side, I could make out an arm, a shoulder, and a few strands of long hair, just enough for me to know it was a girl. The rest of her had been torn away.

I turned the photo over, hoping to find the girl's name written on the back. There was Grandmother's neat, schoolteacherly handwriting: "Gull Cottage, 1977. Dulcie, Claire, and T——."

Like her face, the rest of the girl's name was missing.

Alone in the attic, I stared at the arm and shoulder. *T* . . . Tanya, Tonia, Traci, Terri. So many *T* names to choose from. Which was hers?

Putting the photo back in the book, I ran downstairs to ask Mom about Gull Cottage, the lake, and the girl. I found her in the kitchen chopping onions for the vegetable casserole she was fixing for dinner. Standing there, head down, she wore the same expression caught in the photograph. Not surprising. She always looked sad, even when she wasn't.

I waved the photograph. "Look what I found—a picture of you and Dulcie at a lake somewhere. And another girl——"

Mom snatched the photograph, her face suddenly flushed. "Where did you get this?" She acted as if I'd been rummaging through her purse, her bureau drawers, the medicine cabinet, looking for secrets.

I backed away, startled by her reaction. "It fell out of your old book." I held up *The Bungalow Mystery*. "It was in one of those boxes you brought back from Grandmother's house. Look, here's your name." I pointed to "Claire Thornton, 1977," written in a childish scrawl on the inside cover.

Mom stared at the photograph as if I hadn't spoken. "I was sure I'd thrown this away."

"Who's the girl sitting beside Dulcie?" I asked, unable to restrain my curiosity.

"Me," Mom said without raising her eyes.

"No, I mean on the other side, where it's ripped." I pointed. "See her arm and her shoulder? On the back Grandmother wrote *T*, but the rest of her name was on the torn part."

"I don't remember another girl." Mom gripped the photo and shook her head. "At the lake, it was always Dulcie and me, just Dulcie and me. Nobody else."

At that moment, Dad came through the kitchen door and set a grocery bag on the counter. "Salad stuff," he said. "They didn't have field greens, so I got baby spinach."

"Fine," Mom said.

"What are you looking at?" Reaching over Mom's shoulder, he took the photo. "Little Claire and little Dulcie," he said with a smile. "What a cute pair you were. Too bad the picture's torn— and the color's so awful."

Mom reached for the photo, but Dad wasn't finished with it.

"This must have been taken in Maine," he said.

"Yes." She reached for the picture again.

"Hey, look at this." Dad handed her the photo. "There's another girl sitting next to Dulcie. See her arm? Who was she?"

"This picture was taken thirty years ago," she said sharply. "I have no idea who that girl was."

Slipping the photo into her pocket, Mom went to the kitchen window and gazed at the backyard, which was just beginning to show green after the winter. With her back to us, she said, "Soon it'll be time to mulch the garden."

It was her way of ending the conversation, but Dad chose to ignore the hint. "Your mom and aunt spent their vacations at Sycamore Lake when they were little," he told me. "They still own Gull Cottage, but neither one of them has gone there since they were kids."

"Why not?" I asked. "A cottage on a lake . . . I'd love to see it."

"Don't be ridiculous," Mom said, her back still turned. "The place has probably fallen to pieces by now."

"Why not drive up and take a look this summer?" Dad asked her. "Ali would love Maine—great hiking, swimming, canoeing, and fishing. Lobster, clams, blueberries. We haven't had a real vacation for years."

Mom spun around to face us, her body tense, her voice shrill. "I hated going there when I was little. The lake was cold and deep and scary, and the shore was so stony, it hurt my feet. It rained for weeks straight. Thunder, lightning, wind, fog. The gnats and mosquitoes were vicious. Dulcie and I fought all the time. I never want to see Gull Cottage again. And neither does Dulcie."

"Oh, come on, Claire," Dad said, laughing. "It couldn't have been *that* bad."

"You don't know anything about it." Pressing her fingers to her temples, a sure sign of a headache, she left the room and ran upstairs. A second later, the bedroom door slammed shut.

I turned to Dad, frustrated. "What's the matter with Mom now?"

"Go easy on her, Ali. You know how easily she gets upset." He sighed and headed toward the stairs. "Don't you have a math test tomorrow?"

Alone in the kitchen, I opened my textbook and stared at a page of algebra problems. *Go easy on your mother, don't upset her, she can't handle it.* How often had I heard that? My mother was fragile. She worried, she cried easily, sometimes she stayed in bed for days with migraine headaches.

From the room overhead I could hear the drone of my parents' voices. Mom's voice rose sharp and tearful. "I've told you before, I don't want to talk about it."

Dad mumbled something. I closed my algebra book and retreated to the family room. With the TV on, I couldn't hear them arguing, but even a rerun of *Law and Order* couldn't keep me from thinking about the photo. I certainly hadn't meant to start a scene—I just wanted to know who "T" was.

I never saw the photo again. No one mentioned Sycamore Lake or Gull Cottage. But the more we didn't talk about it, the more I thought about it. Who was "T"? Why didn't Mom remember her? If Grandmother had still been alive, I swear I would've called her and asked who "T" was.

I thought about calling Dulcie and asking her, but if Mom saw the number on the phone bill, she'd want to know why I'd called my aunt and what we'd talked about. Mom had "issues with Dulcie"—her words. They couldn't be together for more than a few hours without arguing. Politics, child raising, marriage— they didn't agree on anything.

Maybe because I couldn't talk to anyone about the photo, I began dreaming about "T" and the lake. Week after week, the same dream, over and over and over again.

I'm walking along the shore of Sycamore Lake in a thick fog. I see a girl coming toward me. I can't make out her face, but somehow I know it's "T." She seems to know me, too. She says, "You'd better do something about this." She points at three girls in a canoe, paddling out onto the lake. One is my mother, one is Dulcie, and I think the third girl is "T." But how can that be? Isn't she standing a few feet away? No, she's gone. The canoe vanishes into the fog.

That's when I always woke up. Scared, shivering—the way people feel when they say, "Someone's walking on my grave."

I wanted to tell Mom about the dream, but I knew it would

upset her. Although Dad didn't agree, it seemed to me she'd been more nervous and anxious since I'd shown her the photograph. She started seeing her therapist again, not once but twice a week. Her headaches came more frequently, and she spent days lying on the couch reading poetry, mainly Emily Dickinson—not a good choice in my opinion for a depressed person. Dickinson's poems were full of things I didn't quite understand but that frightened me. Her mind was haunted, I thought, by death and sorrow and uncertainty. Sometimes I suspected that's why Mom liked Dickinson—they were kindred spirits.

Except for my dream and Mom's days on the couch, life went on pretty much as usual. Dad taught his math classes at the university, graded exams, gave lectures, and complained about lazy students and boring faculty meetings—standard stuff. I got involved in painting scenery for the school play and doing things with my friends. As the weather warmed, Mom cheered up a bit and went to work in her flower garden, mulching, transplanting, choosing new plants at the nursery—the best therapy, she claimed.

And then Dulcie paid us an unexpected visit and threw everything off track.

2

One afternoon in May, I came home from school and found Dulcie and Emma in the living room with Mom. My heart gave a little dance at the sight of my aunt's tall, skinny figure, her fashionably baggy linen overalls, the familiar mop of long tawny curls, the rings on her fingers. Right down to her chunky sandals and crimson toenails, she looked like what she was—an artist.

"Ali!" Dulcie jumped to her feet and crossed the room to hug me. "It's great to see you."

"You, too." I hugged her tightly and breathed in the musky scent of her perfume.

Holding me at arm's length, she gave me a quick once-over. Her silver bracelets jingled. "Look at you—a teenager already." She turned to Mom with a smile. "They grow up so fast!"

"She's only thirteen," Mom murmured. "Don't rush things."

Dulcie frowned as if she might start arguing about how grown up I was. Before she could say anything, though, Emma flung herself at me. "Ali, Ali, Ali!"

"Whoa," I laughed. "You're getting so big, you'll knock me down! Look at your hair—it's almost as long as mine."

Emma giggled and hugged me. "That's 'cause I'm almost five. Soon I'll be as big as you."

Keeping an arm around my cousin's shoulders, I turned back to Dulcie. "Are you in town for a show or—"

"I had to see the owner of a gallery in D.C. She wants to exhibit my work in a group show next fall, and I need peace and quiet to paint, so . . ." Dulcie glanced at Mom who sighed and shook her head, obviously worried about something.

"Your mother thinks this is the worst idea I've ever had," Dulcie went on with a laugh. "But I'm going to fix up the old cottage at the lake and spend the summer there."

I stared at her, hardly daring to believe she was serious. Sycamore Lake, the place that had obsessed me for two months now. Before I could bombard her with questions, Mom said, "Dulcie, I really think—"

"No arguments. My mind's made up." Dulcie smiled at Mom and turned to me. "I need a babysitter to entertain Emma while I paint. I'm trying to talk your mom into letting me borrow you for the summer."

"Me?" My face flushed. "I'd love to baby-sit Emma at the lake! I've wanted to see it for ages. I found a—"

"Ali," Mom interrupted. "I *told* you what it's like there. Rain and mosquitoes and cold, gloomy days. Nothing to do. Nowhere to go. You'll hate it."

"Don't believe a word of it," Dulcie told me. "Sure, it's cold and rainy sometimes. It's Maine—what do you expect? But there's plenty of sunshine. The mosquitoes aren't worse than anyplace else. The lake's—"

"The lake's deep . . . and dark . . . and dangerous," Mom cut in, choosing her words slowly and deliberately. "People drown there every summer."

Dulcie frowned at Mom. "Do you have to be so negative about *everything?*"

To keep Mom from starting a scene, I jumped into the conversation.

8

"I've taken swimming lessons since I was six years old. I know all about water safety. I'd never do anything stupid."

"Please, Aunt Claire, please, please, please!" Emma begged. "I want Ali to be my babysitter." She hopped back and forth from one foot to the other, staring hopefully at Mom.

Say yes, I begged silently, *say yes.* My best friend, Staci, was going away, and a boring summer stretched ahead. I loved Emma, and I loved my aunt. A few months at the lake would be perfect.

Ignoring my pleading look, Mom shook her head. "I can't possibly make a decision until Pete comes home from work. Ali's his daughter, too. We have to agree on what's best for her."

Dulcie dropped onto the sofa beside Mom. "Sorry. I'm used to making my own decisions about Emma." Tossing her hair to the side, she grinned at me. "It's one of the many advantages of being divorced."

"I didn't mean——" Mom said.

"How about some coffee?" Dulcie asked, quickly diverting Mom. "And some fruit juice for Emma?"

"Of course." Mom got up and headed for the kitchen with Dulcie behind her. I trailed after them, but at the doorway, my aunt turned and smiled at me. "Why don't you read to Emma, sweetie? She put some of her favorite books in my bag."

Secrets, I thought. *Things they don't want me to know about.* I was tempted to follow them into the kitchen anyway, but it occurred to me that Dulcie might have better luck talking to Mom without my being there listening to every word.

Emma rummaged through her mother's big straw bag and pulled out *The Lonely Doll,* a book I'd enjoyed when I was little.

"I like when Edith meets the bears, and she isn't lonely anymore." Emma climbed into my lap and rested her head against my shoulder.

"I like that part, too."

Emma opened the book to a photo of Edith looking sad and lonely. "Someday I'll have a friend," she said. "And then I won't be lonely anymore."

"Silly," I said. "You must have friends. Everyone has friends."

She shook her head. "Not in New York. Everybody I know there is grown up. And grownups can't be your friends."

"Can I be your friend? Or am I too old?"

Emma gave me a solemn, considering look. "It would be better if you were five or six or even seven," she said, "but I guess you can be sort of a friend."

"Thank you, Princess Emma." I gave her a little tickle in the side. "I'm greatly honored by your majesty's decision."

She giggled. "Will you read now?"

When we were about halfway through the story, we were distracted by rising voices in the kitchen.

"We're adults now," Mom was saying. "I don't have to do everything you say. Ali's my daughter. I'll raise her the way I see fit!"

"It must be nice to own a child," Dulcie replied.

"'Own a child'? What's that supposed to mean?"

"You're so overprotective, you might as well keep her on a leash. Sit, Ali. Heel, Ali. Roll over, Ali."

"How can you say that?" Mom's voice rose. "I love Ali and I want her to be safe. She's not going to spend the summer running wild, swimming, going out in boats—"

"Don't hold on so tight," Dulcie interrupted. "Ali's growing up. She has to start making her own decisions. It might be good for her to get away from you. She—"

"You always took everything away from me when I was little!"

Mom shouted. "And now you want my own daughter! Can't I have anything?" She started sobbing.

"Oh, that's right," Dulcie said. "Cry when you can't think of anything else to do." There was an edge of cruelty in her voice I'd never heard before. "Grow up, Claire. You're not a little kid anymore."

Emma put her arms around my neck and pressed her face against my chest. "Make them stop, Ali."

The voices in the kitchen dropped so low that I couldn't hear what Mom or Dulcie was saying.

"I think they stopped all by themselves, Emma." I patted her back, but my mind was racing. Dulcie was right. Mom *did* overprotect me; even Staci thought so. She never let me do *anything*—not even spend a night at Staci's house or go the mall with my friends. I really did need to get away from her for a while.

But at the same time I was agreeing with Dulcie, I was feeling bad because she'd upset Mom. I was confused, as well. Why did Mom think Dulcie wanted to take me away from her? What else had she taken? It was enough to give *me* a headache.

Emma nudged me. "Read, Ali. I want to hear the part where Little Bear and Edith play dress-up, and Edith writes, 'Mr. Bear is just a silly old thing!' on the mirror with lipstick and Mr. Bear gets cross." She giggled. "And then Edith calls him a silly and he spanks her and she's scared Mr. Bear will take Little Bear and go away and she'll be lonely again."

"You sure know this story well."

"Edith is lonely like me, and she has blond hair like me, and she lives in an apartment in New York like me. And she wishes so hard for a friend that Mr. Bear and Little Bear come to her house just to be her friends. And that's what I wish for, too. A friend. Somebody who likes me best of all."

I started reading again, and Emma pressed against me, mouthing the words silently as if she knew the story by heart.

While I read, I kept one ear tuned to the kitchen, but I couldn't hear what Mom and Dulcie were saying. If Emma hadn't been sitting on my lap, I would have tiptoed to the door and listened.

3

At the end of the story, Mr. Bear promised Edith he'd stay with her forever.

"'Forever and ever!'" Emma shouted along with Little Bear.

We said the book's last three words together: "'And they did!'"

"When I was little, I wanted a doll just like Edith," I told Emma.

"I want one, too," Emma said, "but Mommy says they're very, very expensive."

I sighed, thinking about things that cost too much to own—a horse, a mountain bike like Staci's, a swimming pool in the back-yard, even a doll. . . .

The front door opened, and Dad stopped at the threshold to grin at Emma, who ran to him.

"What a nice surprise!" Dropping his briefcase, he scooped Emma up and gave her a hug. "Look at you—just as beautiful as your mommy!"

Emma laughed and kissed Dad's nose.

The kitchen door swung open. Mom and Dulcie seemed to have made up after their quarrel, but Mom still looked tense, worried, uneasy.

"It's good to see you, stranger." Dad put Emma down and gave Dulcie a hug and a kiss. It was a long hug, I thought. I glanced at Mom. She was watching the two of them, but I couldn't read her expression—except that I could tell she wasn't happy.

"What brings you here?" Dad asked Dulcie.

"I'm in a group show at a D.C. gallery next fall," Dulcie said. "Emma and I took the train down so I could talk to the owner. Since we were so close, I called Claire, and she picked us up at the station. We're going back to New York tomorrow morning."

Emma grabbed Dad's hand. "Mommy wants Ali to baby-sit me at the lake, but Aunt Claire says she can't."

Dad turned to Dulcie and raised his eyebrows. "Sycamore Lake?"

"I drove to the cottage a couple of weeks ago," Dulcie said. "Considering how long it's been empty, it's in pretty good shape. A couple of broken windows, a few leaks in the roof, and a dozen or more mice nesting in the cupboards."

Dulcie glanced at Mom. "A trap will take care of the mice, and I've hired a contractor to fix everything else. By the time he's done, Gull Cottage will have electricity, indoor plumbing, fresh paint inside and out, a new roof—and the old boathouse will be my studio."

"In other words, it'll be better than new." Dad turned to Mom. "So why can't Ali baby-sit Emma?"

"You know I hate the lake." Mom's voice rose a few notches, tense, anxious. "Ali could drown, she could get Lyme disease from a deer tick, she could get bitten by a snake, she—"

"Oh, for heaven's sake." Ignoring Mom's whimper of protest, Dad looked at me. "How do you feel about the idea, Ali?"

"I want to go," I said. "Staci will be away all summer. I'm sick of the swimming pool and the softball team." *And of Mom watching me all the time,* I wanted to add, *keeping me on a leash, owning me.* Instead, I said, "The lake would be fun—an adventure, something different."

"Please, please, *pretty* please?" Emma begged. "I'll be so lonely without Ali."

14

"Let her go, Claire," Dad said. "She loves Dulcie and Emma. And they love her."

"I'll take good care of Ali," Dulcie put in. "I won't let her or Emma run wild. I promise."

"You'll get absorbed in your painting and forget all about them," Mom muttered.

Dulcie exhaled sharply, clearly exasperated. "I've had sole responsibility for Emma since she was a baby. Does she look neglected?"

The argument went on during dinner, which made it hard to enjoy the pasta topped with Dulcie's special marinara sauce, concocted from her ex-husband's Italian grandmother's recipe.

"It's the only good thing I ever got from that man," Dulcie said. "Besides Emma, of course."

Dad laughed and Mom allowed herself to smile, and then they returned to the argument. Round and round they went, saying the same things over and over again. Mom refused to give in: I was too young to leave home for a whole summer, too young to be responsible for Emma.

At the end of the meal, Dad laid his fork and knife on his plate and said, "I've heard enough. Ali's a sensible, responsible girl. There's absolutely no reason why she shouldn't spend the summer at the lake."

Mom put her coffee cup down and stared at him, obviously shocked. "Pete, please——"

Whatever she was about to say was drowned out by Emma's shout of joy. "Hooray! Hooray!" She jumped up from the table and ran to hug Dad. "Thank you, Uncle Pete, thank you!"

I looked at Mom uneasily, taking in the defeated slump of her shoulders. "Say it's okay," I begged. "Say I can go and you won't be mad." *Or hurt. Or betrayed. Or worried.*

She wiped her mouth carefully with her napkin. "If it means so much to you, go." Without looking at anyone, she rose from the table and began gathering the dinner plates. The set of her jaw and her jerky movements clearly showed her anger.

"Give me a break, Claire. Don't get in one of your moods." Dulcie picked up a few glasses and followed Mom into the kitchen.

Carrying the serving bowls, I trailed after them, with Emma close behind clasping a fistful of spoons and forks. She handed them to Mom, then ran off to the living room.

Without speaking to anyone, Mom began loading the dishwasher.

"It's the silent treatment," Dulcie whispered to me. "She inherited it from our mother—and perfected it."

I turned away, unwilling to criticize Mom. Dulcie was right, of course—silence and tears were Mom's weapons. But it made me uncomfortable to agree with my aunt. After all, I had no reason to complain. I'd won. I was going to Sycamore Lake.

Leaving Mom to clean up, I followed Dulcie into the living room. Dad was reading *The Lonely Doll* to Emma in a sweet bumbling bear voice.

I perched on the arm of Dulcie's chair. "Can I ask you something?"

"Sure, sweetie." Dulcie pushed her hair back from her face. Her long dangly silver earrings swayed and her bracelets jingled. She smiled, waiting for me to speak.

"Well, a couple of months ago I found an old Nancy Drew book in a box in the attic. While I was leafing through it, a photograph fell out. It was of you and Mom at Sycamore Lake—I could see the water behind you."

Dulcie smiled. "Your grandfather loved taking pictures. Every time you turned around, there he was, pointing a camera at you.

They were usually awful. We thought he had a special ugly lens he used for our pictures."

"There was another girl with you," I said, "but all that shows is her shoulder and arm. The rest is torn off."

"Another girl?" Dulcie shook her head, and her soft hair brushed my cheek. "We didn't have any friends at the lake. Gull Cottage sits out on a point, all by itself. There were no other kids around—just your mother and me."

"Grandmother wrote your name and Mom's name on the back," I went on, trying to make her remember. "She wrote the girl's name, too, but only the first letter is still there—'T.'"

"'T'?" An odd look crossed Dulcie's face. "Did you ask your mother about the girl?"

"I told her I didn't remember." Mom stood in the doorway, her hands clasped, staring solemnly at her sister.

"I don't remember, either," Dulcie said quickly.

"What did you do with the picture, Mom? Maybe if Dulcie saw it—"

"I threw it away," she said. "It was old, torn, faded." Without another word, she picked up a gardening book and began to read, her way of saying she was still in a bad mood.

Before I could ask another question, Dulcie scooped up Emma. "Time for bed."

"But Uncle Pete is still reading about Edith and the bears," she said.

"You know that story by heart, sweetheart." Ignoring Emma's further protests, Dulcie carted her off to the guest room.

Dad turned on the TV to watch one of his favorite crime shows. It looked as if no more would be said about "T" that night.

4

After Dulcie and Emma went back to New York, Mom nursed her bad mood for weeks. She refused to take me shopping for summer clothes, so I tagged along with Staci and her mother. She wouldn't talk about the lake or give me any baby-sitting tips. She spent almost all her time working in the garden, down on her hands and knees, weeding till her knuckles bled, watering and fertilizing, rearranging plants, adding new ones. *Just to avoid me,* I thought.

Even Dad found it hard to be patient with her, especially after she changed her mind about driving me to the lake.

"If Dulcie wants Ali to baby-sit, she can pick her up and drive her to Maine herself," she told him.

He stared at her. "But, Claire, what about our plans to spend a few days on the coast?"

"I can't leave the flowers. They'll dry up. The weeds will take over." Mom folded her arms tightly across her chest, her face taut with anxiety.

Dad's frown deepened. "You realize that coming all the way down here to get Ali will add hours to Dulcie's trip."

Mom shrugged. "It was Dulcie's idea to take Ali to the lake. Let her figure it out. She can always find another babysitter."

Close to tears, I glared at Mom. "You're still trying to keep me from going, aren't you? Why don't you just put me on a leash and tie me to a tree in the backyard?"

My outburst surprised Dad, but Mom nodded her head angrily. "You should've been Dulcie's daughter—you're more like her every day."

"Good. Maybe I won't grow up scared of everything, afraid to have fun, ruining everybody else's fun."

Too upset to reply, Mom ended the conversation by leaving the room.

Dad grabbed my shoulders and gave me a little shake, more to get my attention than anything else. "Don't talk to your mother like that. Can't you see you're hurting her?"

I wanted to say Mom was hurting *me,* but Dad had already followed her out of the room. *She's not having a nervous breakdown,* I shouted silently. *She's just crying because she can't think of anything else to do.*

I sighed and grabbed an apple from the bowl on the counter. Living in this house was good practice for crossing a minefield. If you weren't careful, you could set off explosions with every step you took.

While I ate my apple, I stared out the kitchen window at the neighbor's dog, tied to his tree. He lay in the dirt, his nose on his paws—totally bored, I was sure, but safe.

The day I left, Mom refused to get out of bed, claiming she had a migraine, the worst she'd had in over a year. Dad pulled the blinds to darken the room and sat with her for a while, reading a book as she dozed, another way to avoid talking.

When Dulcie arrived, Mom didn't feel well enough to see her, so we said our goodbyes in her bedroom. "You don't have to stay at the lake if you're unhappy or homesick," she whispered. "If anything scares you or worries you, call us. Your father will come get you."

"Don't worry. Everything will be fine," I assured her.

Mom squeezed my hand. "I know you think I'm too protective," she said, "but I want to keep you safe. You're so young. You don't know the terrible things that can happen, how quickly one's life can change."

"What do you mean?"

She closed her eyes. "My head hurts. I can't talk anymore."

I leaned over and kissed her gently. "I'll be careful in the water," I promised, "and I'll take good care of Emma. Please don't worry. I love you and I'll miss you."

Keeping her eyes closed, Mom said, "I love you, too."

On the way downstairs, I asked Dad if the migraine was my fault.

"Of course not," he said. "It's tension, anxiety . . ."

Then it is my fault. I caused the tension and anxiety, didn't I? I pushed the guilty thought away. Mom often had migraines. I couldn't be blamed for all of them. *Maybe this one, though.*

Moments later, Emma was hugging me, squealing with delight, and Dulcie was assuring Dad she'd drive carefully and keep a close eye on me all summer.

Dad wedged my suitcase and bag of books into the van. I belted myself in the front seat, and Dulcie secured Emma in the back seat.

As I waved goodbye to Dad, I thought I saw a hand raise the blind in my parents' bedroom. Mom must have felt well enough to watch her sister take me away for the summer.

The ride to Maine seemed to last forever—one boring interstate after another, dodging trucks, passing cars and motorcycles, stopping a couple of times at fast-food places for hamburgers and fries. Not what she usually ate, Dulcie assured me, but the quickest way to fill our stomachs.

Late in the afternoon, we left the last interstate and followed a network of roads, each narrower and more winding than the one before.

Emma leaned over the seat. "Are we almost there?"

Dulcie nodded. "See that tree? The one with the long limb like a trunk sticking out over the road? Claire and I called it the elephant tree. We'll be at the cottage soon."

A few minutes later, Dulcie slowed down and pointed out a little white store by the side of the road. Its windows were boarded up and a weather-beaten sign over the door said, OLSON'S. Weeds grew in the parking lot, and a row of seagulls perched on the roof.

"Claire and I used to ride our bikes all this way for home-made ice cream—the best chocolate I ever tasted." Dulcie sighed. "Too bad it's closed."

Soon after, she said, "It's the next left, just past that patch in the asphalt that looks like a bear. See? There's the sign for Gull Cottage." She pointed at a neatly lettered arrow-shaped board nailed to a tree. Below it was a mailbox, its door down, empty.

Dulcie turned onto a one-lane dirt road and we headed into the woods. The setting sun shot golden beams through the trees, but the light was dim and greenish, almost as if we were underwater.

We rounded a curve, and there it was, a small cottage sheltered by tall trees. The clapboards had a fresh coat of blue paint, and the steep roof was newly shingled. The lake itself was down a flight of wooden steps. I could see a dock and a small building beside it. Beyond a curve of sandy beach was the water, dark in the early evening light, stretching out to the horizon.

"It looks almost exactly the same," Dulcie said. "Joe did a great job."

With Emma close behind, I followed Dulcie across a deck and through the back door. I don't know exactly what I'd expected—cobwebs and dust, stale air, maybe a gloomy, spooky atmosphere—but the cottage was bright and airy. Blue checked curtains hung at the kitchen windows, and the cabinets had been painted a sunny yellow, the walls pale blue, the table and chairs bright blue. The stove and refrigerator were a brand-new dazzling white.

"The old ones were antiques," Dulcie said. "Plus they didn't work."

She led us into the living room, which was furnished with a pair of soft armchairs and a matching sofa sagging beneath faded flowered slipcovers. A big stone fireplace took up one whole wall, and windows with a view of the lake took up another wall. Shelves full of books and board games covered the third wall from floor to ceiling.

"The cottage was filthy when I saw it in April," Dulcie said. "Joe hired a cleaning crew to scrub and vacuum. They got rid of spiders, squirrels, mice, and a family of raccoons living under the deck."

"But they didn't hurt them, did they?" Emma asked, her voice full of concern.

"Of course not, sweetie. They caught the mice and squirrels and raccoons in Havahart traps and let them go in a nice part of the woods, and they picked up the spiders very gently in tissue and carried them outside."

"That's good." Emma looked pleased. "If they come back, they can sleep in my room. I won't mind."

Dropping her suitcases at the foot of a narrow flight of steps, Dulcie pointed down the hall. "Two bedrooms—one for Emma and one for me. Plus a brand-new bathroom."

My room was upstairs, tucked snugly under the eaves. A faded patchwork quilt in shades of blue, yellow, and green calico covered the double bed. Its iron frame had been painted white to match an old dresser and a table and chair as well as built-in shelves, already holding books and toys. Fresh muslin curtains hung at the windows, and a rag rug covered most of the floor.

"This was your mom's and my room when we were kids," Dulcie said. "Same wallpaper, same furniture."

She picked up a conch shell lying on the bureau and turned it slowly, studying its shape and colors before putting it back. "Our mother left everything here. I guess she thought we'd come back one summer, but we never did."

Her voice had dropped so low, I barely understood what she'd said.

"Why didn't you come back?" I asked. "Did something happen?"

Dulcie stared at me. "Of course nothing happened. Whatever gave you that idea?"

"Mom, I guess. The way she talks about the lake, like it's a scary place." Suddenly embarrassed, I picked up the shell Dulcie had been looking at. "This is really pretty."

"Let me see." Emma reached for the shell, and I handed it to her. She held it as carefully as if it were made of glass and pressed it to her ear. "I hear the ocean," she whispered.

Dulcie looked at me over Emma's head. "Everything scares Claire," she said. "Deep water. High places, low places. Inside, outside. Upside, downside."

Even though I'd often thought the same thing, Dulcie's tone of voice stung. Mom was lying in bed at home, sick, in pain, while I'd traveled all this way without her. "She can't help it. She worries, that's all."

Dulcie shrugged. "To answer your question, I guess we didn't come back because we got tired of coming here. For kids, there's not a whole lot to do. We spent our summers traveling instead—Yellowstone, the Grand Canyon, Yosemite, Niagara Falls, the Canadian Rockies." She laughed. "Dad did a lot of driving in those years."

Emma picked up one of a pair of teddy bears sitting in a small rocking chair. "He looks just like Mr. Bear," she said.

"He belonged to Claire," Dulcie said. "And that's just what she called him. Mr. Bear."

"That's the bear's name in *The Lonely Doll*. Mr. Bear and Little Bear, the friends Edith wishes so hard for." Emma hugged the bear. "If I wish hard enough, will a friend come?"

Dulcie leaned down to kiss Emma's cheek. "Just wait till you start kindergarten in the fall. You'll have so many friends, you won't have to wish." She smoothed her daughter's silky hair back from her face, tucking it behind her ears.

"Does Mr. Bear belong to you now?" Emma asked me.

"You can have him," I told her. "I think he likes you best of all."

Emma grinned and hugged the bear. "And you can have the other one."

"He was mine." Dulcie picked up the bear, a sad companion to Mom's. His fur was almost worn off, stuffing leaked from one paw, and he was missing an eye.

"Poor old thing," Dulcie said. "Claire took good care of her toys, but I was rough on everything—toys, clothes, books. Even people."

She sighed and gave the bear a hug. "His name is Rufus M., after the little boy in the Moffat Family books." Dropping the bear on the foot of the bed, she stretched. "I guess it's time to start dinner."

5

When Dulcie was gone, Emma sat on the bed and watched me put my things into the bureau drawers. "Is Aunt Claire mad at Mommy?" she asked. "Is that why she didn't come down to see us before we left?"

I shook my head. "My mom gets awful headaches," I told Emma. "They're called migraines. When she has a really bad one, she stays in bed and doesn't talk to anyone."

"Poor Aunt Claire." Emma stroked Mr. Bear's fur. "I'll make her a get-well card tomorrow. It'll be from me and Mr. Bear. Would she like that?"

I grinned. "She'd *love* a card, especially from you."

Emma looked at me thoughtfully. "Aunt Claire doesn't like the lake, does she? She almost didn't let you come with me and Mommy."

I opened the casement window and leaned out to look at the water. The evening star hung low in the sky, kept company by a half-moon, but it was still light enough to make out the horizon, a dark line against the fading pink of the sunset.

"My mom's scared of water," I said. "I've never seen her go swimming. Not once. Even when she took me to the pool for lessons, she sat on the grass and watched me. All the other mothers were in the water with their kids. But not my mother."

Beside me, Emma shuddered. "Maybe she thinks she'll drown. She doesn't want her bones to come out."

I looked at her. "What are you talking about?"

"Bones are inside us, you and me and Mommy and everybody. When we die they come out, and then we're ghosts."

"Where did you get that idea?"

"I saw pictures in Mommy's drawing books. She said they're skeletons. We all have them inside—until we die, and then . . ." Emma hugged Mr. Bear. "He doesn't have bones, just stuffing. And he's not alive, so he can't die. Or be a ghost."

"There's no such thing as ghosts."

Emma turned her hands this way and that, as if observing the movement of the bones under her skin. "How do you know? Maybe you just haven't seen one."

"Don't be a Silly Billy." I forced myself to laugh. "Of course I haven't seen a ghost. And neither have you."

"I've seen one in my dreams." Emma spoke so softly I had to lean down to hear her. "The ghost is very sad and lonely. She wants to go home, but she's down deep, deep, deep in the water. She's been there so long, she's just bones. No one knows where she is."

Emma's whispery voice made my skin race with goose bumps. I pulled her small body close to mine and hugged her. Mr. Bear's fur tickled my nose. "That's very scary," I told her, "but it's just a bad dream. Everybody has them."

Emma peered into my eyes. "Do you?"

I thought about "T." I hadn't dreamt about her for weeks— until last night. I must have been worried about coming to the lake, leaving Mom, all that. I hoped I wouldn't dream about her now that I was actually here.

"Not very often," I fibbed to keep from alarming Emma.

While we'd been talking, the room had darkened. Shadows gathered in the corners, and a cool breeze fluttered the curtains.

26

Somewhere outside a bird cried once . . . twice . . . three times.

I took Emma's hand and led her toward the stairs. "Let's go see what your mom's doing."

In the brightly lit kitchen, Emma ran to Dulcie. "Mr. Bear wants dinner," she said, waving him at her mother. "He's hungry."

Dulcie gave her a kiss. "It's almost ready. Why don't you and Ali set the table? The forks and knives and spoons are in that drawer." She pointed to the cabinet by the sink, and Emma began counting out the utensils—four of each.

"There's only three of us," I said.

"You forgot Mr. Bear." Emma sat the teddy in the extra chair and laid a fork, knife, and spoon in front of him.

I laughed a little louder than I'd meant to, in relief, I guess, that Mr. Bear was joining us . . . not the ghost from Emma's dream.

Dulcie brought over a big yellow bowl of spaghetti and set it down in the middle of the table. "The sauce isn't as good as my ex-mother-in-law's," she said, "but it's not bad with plenty of parmesan sprinkled on top."

She tucked a napkin around Emma's neck and served us each a heaping portion.

"Don't forget Mr. Bear," Emma said. "He hasn't had anything to eat for years and years and years."

Dulcie put a small amount on a saucer and set it in front of the bear. "Eat up," she told him. "I don't like bears who waste food."

After dinner, Dulcie lit a fire. Emma and I sprawled on the rug and roasted marshmallows. I let mine turn black on the outsides and sucked the gooey white insides into my mouth. "Yum."

"Ugh," said Emma. She liked hers barely toasted, but Dulcie burned hers even blacker than mine.

We washed the marshmallows down with hot chocolate, then lay still and watched the flames devour the logs. Our faces felt warm, but our feet were cold.

On the sofa, Dulcie sighed happily and stretched her long legs toward the fire. "I'd forgotten how chilly Maine gets at night," she said. "We'll need extra blankets. And cozy flannel jammies."

Emma yawned and rubbed her eyes.

"Look like someone's ready for bed." Dulcie scooped her up and gave her a hug. "Let's go, sleepyhead."

"You come, too." Emma stretched her arms toward me. "And bring Mr. Bear. He's scared of the dark."

Carrying the bear, I followed Dulcie and Emma to the small room at the back of the cottage. As soon as Emma was ready for bed, she found *The Lonely Doll* and handed it to Dulcie. "Read this one."

"But I read that book last night and the night before and the night before that—"

"It's my favorite," Emma insisted. She climbed into bed and tucked the bear under the covers beside her. "I bet Ali wants to hear it—don't you?"

"Sure." I stretched out on the bed beside Emma and listened to Dulcie begin the story.

After she'd read a few pages, Emma interrupted her. "It's so dark outside my window. Why aren't there any lights or any people? I don't even hear any cars."

"We're out in the country now, Em, where it's peaceful and quiet."

"Will you pull down the shades so I don't have to see the dark? Ghosts could be out there, watching me."

Before Dulcie could move, I jumped up and shut out the night with a few yanks on the blinds. Emma was right. It *was* dark out there. Very dark. No lights anywhere. No sounds but the lapping of the lake against the shore and the wind in the treetops. The cottage was spooky at night, dark, full of shadows, not at all the way it was in the daytime.

"There," I said. "Is that better?"

"I guess so." Emma's voice was low, almost a whisper. She held Mr. Bear tightly. "Read, Mommy."

Dulcie read three *Lonely Doll* books, as well as *The Cat in the Hat, The Cat in the Hat Comes Back, Horton Hatches the Egg,* and *The Owl and the Pussycat.* But it was *Goodnight Moon* that finally lulled Emma to sleep.

Leaving a night-light glowing, Dulcie tiptoed out of the room, and I followed. She closed the door softly and leaned against it for a moment.

"Let's hope Emma adjusts to nights in the wilderness quickly," she said. "I could barely stay awake to read those books."

She yawned and gave me a hug. "I'm beat from all that driving, Ali. I'm going to put out the fire and get into bed."

More tired than I'd realized, I climbed the stairs to my room. Trying to ignore the darkness beyond the bedside lamp, I snuggled under Great-Grandmother's quilt and opened *To Kill a Mockingbird,* number one on my school's summer reading list. I'd seen the movie, but I'd never read the novel. Dad said the book was even better than the movie, but Mom said nothing could beat Gregory Peck as Atticus Finch.

My bed faced the casement windows, slightly open to the cool night air. Through the pine branches, I could see the moon, tipped into a crooked smile. Insects chirped, an owl hooted, the pines sighed in the breeze, and the lake washed against the shore.

With Rufus M. tucked in beside me, I tried to read, but after half an hour, I gave up. It wasn't the book. I loved the story, and I loved the way Harper Lee wrote. I simply couldn't stay awake another second.

I closed my eyes, expecting to fall asleep immediately. But the moon shone in my face. In the woods, the orchestra of insects chirped and thrummed and buzzed, louder and louder.

I found myself thinking of Mom and Dulcie, sharing this bed when they were younger than I was. Had they talked and giggled together? Or had they quarreled the way they did now?

I hugged Rufus. "If you could talk, you'd tell me," I whispered to the old bear. "You were there."

His glass eye glittered in the moonlight, giving him a slightly wicked look. But if the bear knew anything about those long-ago summers, he wasn't telling. Like Mom and Dulcie, Rufus M. knew how to keep secrets.

6

It rained during the night. In the morning it was still coming down, darkening the lake to black and blurring the trees. The air smelled like wet earth and old leaves. A squirrel perched on the deck's railing, his droopy tail wet and pitiful. A few sparrows hopped about here and there, looking almost as wretched as the squirrel.

After breakfast, Dulcie handed out umbrellas and led Emma and me down the steps to the dock. Flinging open the door of the small shingled building, she said, "My studio. Isn't it marvelous?"

Large skylights let in the gray light of the rainy day. Blank canvases leaned against the walls, primed and ready to paint. A long table ran along the back wall, holding paints and brushes, stacks of drawing paper, and books. Above it, built-in shelves bulged with more art supplies and books.

A wood stove and a couch draped with a faded paisley print bedspread occupied one corner, along with a couple of well-worn easy chairs and the potter's wheel Dulcie used to make bowls, mugs, and platters.

I breathed in the smells of paint, turpentine, and linseed oil mingled with lake water and damp, mossy woods. "It's perfect," I said. "I want one just like it!"

Dulcie smiled and pointed to an easel in the middle of the studio. "What do you think of my latest?"

I stared at the large oil, washed in shades of blues, greens, and grays, splashed with flashes of yellow and white. "It makes me think of water."

Dulcie grinned. "It's the first of a series based on the lake and its moods." She turned to the window and stared at the water, dull and gray in the rain. "I want to capture the power in water and rocks and trees—capture it as it captures me." She stood silently for a few moments, toying with a long strand of curly hair. Almost as an afterthought, she added, "Maybe I'll manage to free myself."

I wasn't sure what she meant or even if she were talking to me, so I simply nodded.

"Mommy, can I show Ali my pictures?" Emma asked.

Without looking at either of us, Dulcie said, "Of course. Your folder's on the table."

Emma carefully untied the strings holding her folder closed and began spreading pictures on the table. "I made these in New York," she explained, "and the moving truck brought them here, just like it brought Mommy's paintings."

I looked at the array of rainbows, birds, suns, and flowers, painted in bright reds, yellows, greens, and blues. In some, people with huge smiling faces and long stick arms and legs floated just above the ground. She'd printed her name in big sloppy letters across the top of every picture.

"These are great, Emma. I love the bright colors and all the happy people."

"I'm going to be an artist when I grow up," Emma said, "just like Mommy."

"Me, too. We'll all three be artists together."

Emma clapped her hands. "And this will be where we paint— all three of us. And we'll live together in the cottage. And we won't be lonely."

Dulcie had finally left the window and was now mixing paints on her palette. A new canvas faced her. As she lifted her brush to make the first splash of color, she turned to Emma and me. "Would you girls like to paint, too?"

Emma grabbed a box of tempera paints and handed it to me. "You open the jars," she said, "and I'll get the paper and the brushes."

Soon all three of us were absorbed in painting. Rain pelted the skylights, the lake slapped the shore, the wind blew. Dulcie's CD player was loaded with classical music, Bach and Mozart—or was it Haydn? Well, no matter who it was, the music was perfect, and so was the rain and the wind and the sound of the little waves.

I watched Dulcie wash her canvas with thin layers of color in grayed shades of blue and purple and green: a rainy day at the lake. I tried doing the same thing with the tempera paint, but my brush was too wet. The colors ran and pooled and wrinkled the paper.

"Look, Ali." Emma held up a painting as blotchy and runny as mine, its colors mainly dark blues and blacks with a blob of white.

"Is that the lake on a rainy day?" I asked.

Emma looked at her painting. "Yes, but it's got something else." She pointed to the white blob. "This is a skeleton ghost. See? Here's its head."

Dulcie took the picture and looked at it intently. "What gave you the idea to paint a ghost in the water?"

Emma shrugged. "It's something I dream about." Her voice sank to a whisper. "Bones in the water, bones that come out and chase me."

The studio was so quiet, I could hear raindrops splash against the skylights. A cold draft slipped under the door and wrapped around my ankles. I shivered.

Emma hugged Dulcie. "Don't be mad, Mommy."

Dulcie stared at Emma. "Why would I be mad?"

Emma stroked Dulcie's sleeve. "I don't know."

Dulcie laid the picture on a stack of paper on the table and picked Emma up. "How about painting a rainbow and a smiling sun and a flower?" she asked. "Can you do that for me?"

"I already did lots of those, Mommy." Emma picked up her pictures and sorted through them. "One rainbow, two rainbows, three rainbows," she said. "And here's you and me sitting under a rainbow, and here's one flower, two flowers, four, five, seven flowers."

Dulcie looked at them. "Very nice," she said. "Much better than bones in the lake, don't you think?"

"I guess." Emma went to the window and looked out at the lake. "I wish the rain would go away."

"Me, too." I joined her and frowned at the dark clouds over the dark water. In the glass, I saw Dulcie's reflection behind me. She was sitting at the table, staring at the ghost picture. The expression on her face made me uneasy.

That afternoon, I read to Emma until she fell asleep. While she was napping, Dulcie came in from the studio and made a pot of tea for us. We sat at the kitchen table, warm and snug and dry. Rain gurgled in the downspouts, poured from the eaves, and ran down the windowpanes in large drops.

"Emma has an amazing imagination," I said.

"Sometimes I think she spends too much time alone," Dulcie said slowly. "I wonder if it's good for her."

"I'm an only child, too," I said. "It might be nice to have a

brother or sister, but I'm perfectly happy the way things are."
Except for Mom, I thought. *If only she was like you—never depressed, no headaches, full of energy, going places, doing things.* I stopped myself, guilt stricken.

Dulcie opened a tin of fancy cookies and offered me one. They were thin and crisp, smelled lovely, and tasted even better. Given the opportunity, I could have eaten every one and not left a crumb.

"In New York, we live in a neighborhood with lots of artists but not many kids," Dulcie went on, talking to me as if I was her age, her equal, not a little kid. "I've kept her at home because I can't afford preschool."

"She'll be in kindergarten this fall, won't she?"

Dulcie nodded. "Maybe she'll make friends then."

"Of course she will." I took another cookie. "And this summer she'll have me to play with."

Dulcie smiled and patted my hand. "I'm so glad Claire decided to let you come."

"She almost didn't."

Dulcie shrugged. "Your mom worries too much."

"Has she always been like she is now?"

"Pretty much." Dulcie sighed. "Our mom overprotected her—said she was 'sensitive, delicate, sickly.'"

"Was she?"

"I don't know. I was just a kid myself." Dulcie peered into her teacup as if the answer might be there. "Every time we had a fight, it was my fault. I got blamed for everything." She looked at me. "Sometimes I think Claire played it up to get attention."

Shocked by Dulcie's unkind words, I leapt to Mom's defense. "She has horrible migraines, and she's always feeling bad. Grandmother was probably right about her."

"I know, I know. Believe me, I know." With that, Dulcie gathered the empty teacups and carried them to the sink. "I have to get back to the studio. Please fix Emma a snack when she wakes up. Cookies and juice. Not too much, though, or she won't want dinner."

I jumped up and followed Dulcie to the door. "Are you mad at me? Did I say the wrong thing?"

She gave me a quick hug. "I had no business criticizing your mom. We're just so different, you know? It's hard for us to get along. Always has been."

I watched Dulcie leave the cottage and pause at the top of the steps. She stood there for a few minutes, staring out across the lake. The rain had stopped, but the water was still dark under the gray sky. The wind tugged at her hair, pulling curly strands from her ponytail. She looked small against the churning clouds.

I went back to reading *To Kill a Mockingbird*. After a while, Emma came into the kitchen, still sleepy from her nap. I closed my book and fixed her a glass of juice and a couple of cookies. Outside the rain started falling again and the wind blew. I began to worry Mom had been right about the weather.

That night, Emma's screams woke me from my own dream about "T" and the girls in the canoe. I sat straight up in bed, clutching the covers. Downstairs, Dulcie's footsteps hurried to Emma's room. I ran to the top of the stairs just in time to see her open Emma's door.

"Emma, what's wrong?" she asked.

"The bones came out of the lake," Emma cried. "They're going to get me!"

"It's okay, sweetie, it's okay." Dulcie's voice shook as if

Emma's dream had frightened her, too. "There aren't any bones in the lake. You were dreaming."

I leaned over the railing. "Is she all right?"

In the hall below, Dulcie hugged Emma tight. "She had a bad dream. A nightmare."

Emma looked up at me, still frightened. "The bones came out," she sobbed. "The bones came out."

For a moment, I had a scary feeling that someone else was in the cottage—unseen, watching, waiting. I looked behind me, into the shadowy corners of my room. No one was there, but I couldn't get rid of the feeling or the goose bumps on my arms.

Dulcie smiled up at me. "Everything's all right, Ali. Go back to bed. You look cold."

As Dulcie carried Emma to her room, I wished I could run down the steps and squeeze into the big double bed with them. But that would have been way too babyish. After Dulcie's door closed, I went to my room and snuggled under Great-Grandmother's quilt, shivering with cold.

In my head, Emma's words repeated themselves like a song you can't get out of your mind. *"The bones came out, the bones came out, the bones came out."*

Without wanting to, I pictured skeletons wading out of the dark water and creeping toward the house, their bony arms outstretched. Outside, trees rustled in the breeze, and sticks snapped as if crushed under bony feet. Inside, the floors and steps creaked as if those same bony feet were tiptoeing through the house, upstairs and down, searching the rooms.

Holding Rufus tight, I curled into a ball and willed myself to sleep, but Emma's little voice went on saying, *"The bones came out, the bones came out."*

❧ 7 ❧

The next morning, the lake was gray under heavy clouds. The pines were blurred by mist, but the rain had stopped, and the air smelled clean and fresh.

It was too chilly for swimming but not too cold for a walk along the shore. Emma and I each put on a sweatshirt and jeans, and strolled by the lake. The sandy beach turned to stones not long after we passed the boathouse. I was glad I'd taken Dulcie's advice and worn sandals. If I'd gone barefoot, I'd have been hobbling along like an old lady.

While Emma ran ahead, I gathered stones. They were smooth and round, in shades of pale green, pink, gray, and black. I had an idea I might do something artistic with them, put them in ceramic bowls, maybe, and add driftwood and seagull feathers. I could make the bowls myself and sell my arrangements in gift shops. I'd learn how to throw clay on Dulcie's pottery wheel, I'd mix glazes, I'd use the kiln behind the studio.

I was thinking so hard, I almost walked right past Emma. To my surprise, she was standing beside a stranger, a girl who appeared to be nine or ten years old but small for her age. Her hair was white blond, her eyes were the same gray as the lake, and her skin was a deep tan. Despite the chilly weather, she wore a faded blue bathing suit.

"This is Sissy," Emma said. "I just met her, but she wants to be friends."

Sissy looked at me slantwise, as if she were sizing me up. Would I be good to know? Was I nice? Was I bossy? I gave her the same look. There was something about her I disliked on sight—a sharpness in her eyes, a mean set to her mouth. She was the type who'd lie and get you in trouble.

"This is Ali," Emma told Sissy. "She's my cousin, and she's staying here with Mommy and me. Mommy's an artist, so Ali takes care of me while Mommy paints. She's not a babysitter because I'm not a baby."

Sissy continued to stare at me. "Where's *your* mother?" she asked. Her voice was too high pitched to be easy on the ears.

"In Maryland," I told her. "Where we live. She didn't want to come."

"Why not?" Sissy asked.

Something in her voice, a sassiness I didn't like, annoyed me. "I don't know what business it is of yours." It was a huffy thing to say. Rude, even. But somehow it was her fault I'd said it.

Sissy shrugged, and her shoulder blades jutted out like wings. "I was just wondering. Since when is that a crime?"

Emma laughed uncertainly, not sure if Sissy was joking or not. "Aunt Claire doesn't like the lake. That's why she didn't come."

"Is she scared of water or something?" A breeze from the lake blew Sissy's hair in her face, and she smoothed it behind her ears.

Emma glanced at me as if she thought I'd answer. "I think so," she said uncertainly. "But I'm not."

"I'm not, either." Sissy looked at me. "I bet *she's* scared—just like her mother."

I stopped trying to ignore her. "Back home I'm on the swim team. I've won more trophies than anybody in my class."

"Do you think I care?" Sissy turned to Emma. "Let's build castles."

Emma dropped to her knees beside Sissy, and the two of them began heaping up stones, blond heads together as if they'd been friends forever. I hated to admit it, but I felt left out. Emma was my cousin, my friend, and here she was trying to impress a bratty stranger.

"Are your parents renting a cottage around here?" I asked Sissy, hoping she'd say yes, we're leaving tomorrow, you'll never see me again.

Without looking up from her pile of stones, she said, "I live here."

"Where?" Emma asked.

Sissy pointed. "That way."

Emma peered down the shore. "I don't see a house."

"I walked a long way," Sissy said with a shrug.

"Can we come see you and play at your house sometime?"

Sissy shrugged again. "Maybe."

"We have sand at our beach," Emma went on. "We can build good castles there. Want to come home with us?"

"Not today." Sissy stood up and kicked her pile of stones. Down it tumbled.

"Why'd you do that?" Emma asked.

"It wasn't any good." Sissy scooped up a handful of stones and watched them run through her fingers, *clickety-click*. "I have to go. See you later."

She turned to leave, but Emma ran in front of her, blocking her way. "Will you be here tomorrow, Sissy?"

"Maybe." Dodging Emma, she walked away, her skinny back arrow straight, her skinny arms swinging, her skinny legs zipping along beside the water. Her silky hair floated around her head, lifted by the breeze. She didn't look back. Not once. Soon the mist swallowed her up.

When Sissy was out of sight, Emma took my hand. "Do you think she likes me?"

"Everybody likes you." I swung Emma's hand as we walked. "Do you like her?"

"Of course. Don't you?"

"Not especially."

"Why not?"

"I don't know. I guess we aren't, well, very copacetic."

"Cope-a-what?"

"Copacetic. It means getting along with somebody." I was pleased with myself for remembering one of my favorite vocabulary words.

"Well, Sissy's very copacetic with me." Emma broke away and ran along the edge of the water, singing a *Sesame Street* song.

I followed slowly, thinking about the very un-copacetic Sissy. There was something about her I didn't trust. Maybe it was her way of looking past you, not at you. Maybe it was her way of never quite answering questions. The frown on her face didn't help. It wouldn't hurt her to smile once in a while.

"Come on," Emma called. "Catch me!"

I ran after her and picked her up, pretending I was going to toss her into the lake. She shrieked and giggled and broke away from me again. I let her think she'd escaped and then caught her. It was a game Emma never tired of playing.

At lunch, Emma told Dulcie about her new friend. "Her name's Sissy."

"Where does she live?" Dulcie asked.

Emma shrugged. "Around here somewhere."

Dulcie looked puzzled. "I didn't think *anyone* lived around here."

"She said her house was that way." I pointed in what I thought was the right direction.

"She walked a long way," Emma put in. "And all she was wearing was a bathing suit."

"On a day like this? Brr." Dulcie wrapped her sweater tighter around her skinny body and sipped her coffee. "Did Sissy tell you her last name?"

Emma and I shook our heads.

"When you see her again, ask her. Maybe I knew her family from when I was a kid. She probably lives up the road in Webster's Cove."

"Can we go there and see her?" Emma asked.

"Without knowing her last name, how would you find her house?" I asked Emma, glad to think of a reason for not seeing Sissy.

"We could walk around and look for her. Maybe she'd be playing in her yard or something."

"Webster's Cove is a small place, but I doubt you'll find Sissy that way." Dulcie gathered up the dishes and carried them to the sink. "I'm going to the studio now. Be sure and take your nap, Emma. Otherwise, you'll be a crab tonight."

Emma held up her hands like little claws. "Watch out, I'll pinch you, Mommy."

Much to Emma's disappointment, we didn't see Sissy the next day or the day after or the day after that. I didn't mind a bit. The clouds had vanished, and the sun shone. It was perfect weather for swimming, but Emma said the water was too cold. While I practiced my backstroke, she sat on the sand and made castles. Like Sissy, she kicked them down before we left the beach. "No good," she said in a good imitation of her so-called friend.

At the end of the week, Emma suggested walking to Webster's Cove. "Mommy said Sissy might live there, remember? Maybe we'll see her and we can ask her to come home with us and have lunch."

"It's a long way," I said. "If you get tired, I'm not carrying you."

"I won't get tired. I'm big now."

It was about a forty-minute walk, but Emma didn't complain once. She trotted along beside me, talking about Sissy, Sissy, Sissy. What was her favorite color? Did she like chocolate or vanilla ice cream? Did she have sisters or brothers? What TV show did she like best—*Sesame Street* or *Mister Rogers' Neighborhood*? Was she afraid of the dark? Did she have bad dreams? Did she like pizza with extra cheese? Did she have a pet—a cat, a dog, a guinea pig? What did she eat for breakfast—Rice Krispies, Cheerios, Cap'n Crunch?

Emma had so many questions, I almost felt sorry for Sissy.

Webster's Cove was bigger than Dulcie remembered. Cars with out-of-state license plates jammed the narrow streets. People mobbed a little boardwalk running along the edge of the sand. Beach umbrellas tipped this way and that, almost hiding the water. The air smelled of popcorn and suntan lotion and French fries. Kids ran in and out of the lake, shouting and splashing, while their parents watched from folding chairs and blankets.

Emma tugged my arm. "I don't see Sissy."

"It would be hard to find anybody under seven feet tall in this crowd."

Taking her hand, I led her down the boardwalk and into Smoochie's Ice Cream Shop. Maybe the chocolate wouldn't be as good as Olson's, but it would be just as cold and sweet.

I pulled a five-dollar bill out of my pocket. "What would you like?" I asked Emma. "A soda? Ice cream? Candy?"

"Can I have a soda *and* ice cream?"

I checked the price board. I had enough for two small cones and two small sodas. "What flavor do you want?"

Emma pressed her nose against the glass and studied the choices. After several changes of mind, she settled for chocolate and a ginger ale. I picked mint chocolate chip and a root beer.

While we were waiting, Emma peered up at the teenage girl scooping the ice cream. A tag on her polo shirt said her name was Erin.

"Do you know a girl named Sissy?" Emma asked.

Without looking up, Erin said, "Can't say I do."

"She's ten going on eleven and she has long blond hair and she's pretty," Emma went on.

Skinny and mean-eyed, I felt like adding. *Not very nice and not really pretty.*

Erin smiled at Emma. "Sorry, but I don't know her. Maybe her family's here on vacation."

"She lives here," Emma persisted. "All year round."

"I live here all year, too, but I don't know anyone named Sissy. Are you sure she lives in the Cove?"

"No," I put in. "It was just a guess."

Erin handed us our cones and drinks. "There are loads of cottages scattered around the lake," she said. "She could live anywhere."

"I think it's near our cottage," Emma said.

Erin rang up the sale and took my money. While she made change, she asked, "Where do you live?"

"Gull Cottage, down on the Point."

She stared at me. "You're kidding! Nobody's lived there

for ages. Not since——" She frowned and handed me my change.

"Since what?" I asked.

"Huh?"

"You said nobody's lived there 'since.' And then you stopped."
I licked my ice cream. "What were you going to say?"

Erin shrugged and brushed a few stray strands of sun-streaked hair behind her ear. Without looking at me, she said, "Since about thirty years ago. The people who owned it came every summer, but then one year they didn't come back. The cottage has just sat there empty all these years."

"Do you mean the Thorntons?" I asked her.

Erin nodded. "I think that was their name."

"Well, they're back now," I told her. "At least my aunt Dulcie is."

"Really?" Erin stared at me as if she didn't believe me. "Dulcie Thornton's here?"

"That's my mommy's name," Emma said. "She's an artist. Do you know her?"

"Of course not. How old do you think I am?" Erin leaned over the counter until she was face to face with Emma. "But my mom knew Dulcie when they were kids. They used to play together all the time. I think she had a little sister, too."

"Yes," I said. "Claire. That's my mother."

Erin studied Emma and me as if she was memorizing every detail of our appearance—our clothes, our hair, our faces, even how many freckles we had. Her scrutiny made me uncomfortable. Did she think we were strange? Was there something weird about us?

"I'll tell Mom that Dulcie's back," she said at last. "She'll be really interested."

Struck by a sudden thought, I took a deep breath. "What's

45

your mother's name?" I was hoping she'd say Toni or Terri or some other name that started with a *T,* but no luck.

"Jeanine," Erin said. "Jeanine Donaldson, but her maiden name was Reynolds. I know she'll want to see Dulcie. She still talks about her and Claire and what—"

Just then a man herded a couple of cross, sunburned children into the shop. "Two vanilla ice cream cones, please," he said. "Small. And one large diet Sprite."

"I want strawberry," the boy wailed.

"You said vanilla."

"No, no! Strawberry, I want strawberry!"

"Make that one vanilla and one strawberry," the man said. "And an extra-large diet Sprite for me."

"Can we go now?" Emma tugged at my T-shirt. "Maybe Sissy's waiting at home for us."

I waved goodbye to Erin, and we began the long trudge home. The further we walked, the hotter we got. The sun beat on our heads and shoulders, and our clothes stuck to us. Even wading in the lake didn't cool us off.

Before we'd gone halfway, Emma asked me to carry her.

"You promised you'd walk," I reminded her.

"I'm tired," Emma said, close to tears.

"Okay, but just a little way." I picked her up and carried her piggyback style. "Thank goodness you're a little skinny old thing," I told her.

"I'm just a bag of bones," Emma whispered into my ear. After that, she was so quiet I suspected she'd fallen asleep, worn out from the walk. I was pretty tired myself.

When we were almost home, I thought I saw Sissy watching us from a stone jetty poking out into the lake. I didn't wave. Neither did she. She just stood there as still as a heron waiting for a fish. But she was very far away, small in the distance. I could have been mistaken.

At any rate, I was glad Emma didn't see her.

8

In the end, I carried Emma as far as the studio. I lowered her to the ground and woke her up. "You'll have to climb the steps yourself."

The studio door opened, and Dulcie rushed out as if she'd been waiting for us. "Where have you been? You've been gone for ages!"

"We walked to Webster's Cove," I told her. "Emma wanted to find Sissy's house."

Emma threw her arms around Dulcie and burst into tears. "We didn't see Sissy anywhere, and I got so tired and hot."

"We stopped at Smoochie's," I told Dulcie. "The girl who works there, Erin, didn't know Sissy, but she said her mother knows you and Mom. She used to play with you when she was little."

"What was her name?"

"Jeanine something—I forget."

Most people would have paused to think about the name. Not Dulcie. Her answer was quick and sharp. "I don't remember her."

"But she remembers you."

Dulcie frowned and shook her head. "Next time you sashay off to Webster's Cove, please let me know."

I wanted to ask if she had a memory problem, but the grumpy look on her face silenced me.

"It's past time for lunch. Emma must be starved." Dulcie loped up the steps, and Emma and I followed, too tired to keep up with her long legs.

After we ate, Dulcie returned to the studio, and Emma settled down on the couch beside me.

"Will you read this to me?" Emma held up *The Moffats*. "I want to know about Rufus M."

Like most of the things in the cottage, the book was old. The cover was faded, and the pages had a soft, pulpy feel. My grandmother had scrawled her name on the title page, followed by the date June 5, 1945. Under it, Dulcie had written her name and June 2, 1977. Mom added her name the next year. It looked as if another name had been scribbled there, but someone had erased it. All that remained were a few faint pencil marks, impossible to read.

By the time I finished the first chapter, Emma was fast asleep. I lay on my side next to her, tired from our long walk. A fly buzzed against the window screen. The lake lapped the shore. After resting for a while, I went to my room and put on my bathing suit. Leaving Emma to her nap, I ran down the steps to the lake.

Before I waded into the water, I stopped by the studio. Dulcie was sitting on a stool, staring at an unfinished painting, another canvas washed with blues and grays and green. "Where's Emma?" she asked.

"Asleep. Is it okay if I go for a swim?"

Dulcie hesitated. For a moment I was afraid she'd say no. Mom would have. "Promise to stay out of deep water, and be careful." She dipped her brush into blue paint. "Be back in a half-hour or so."

I leaned against the door for a moment and watched Dulcie go to work on the painting. She was soon absorbed in adding daubs of dark blues and blacks.

Completely forgotten, I slipped outside and walked down to the lake. The water was so clear, I could see my toes and the pebbles on the bottom as if I were looking through glass. Schools of silver minnows darted in and out of clumps of grass, turning this way and that in perfect unison, tickling my legs as they swam past.

I waded through knee-deep water, watching the minnows. Every now and then I glimpsed bigger fish—trout, maybe—but they disappeared before I got a good look at them. Seagulls dipped and circled overhead, and the pine forest behind me rang with the cries of crows. The trees made the air smell like Christmas.

I was enjoying myself until I saw Sissy at the end of our stretch of sandy beach. Unaware I was near, she bent over a pile of sand, patiently shaping it into a castle with turrets. I watched her for a few moments, glad Emma was safely at home.

When Sissy began to dig a moat, I splashed out of the water. "Well, well, where have you been?"

She looked up, startled. "What's it to you?"

"Nothing," I said. "It's not like I missed you or anything."

Sissy frowned, her eyes narrowed against the sun. "Where's Emma?"

"Taking a nap." I sat down, scooped up a handful of sand, and watched it trickle slowly through my fingers.

"It's boring to sleep." Sissy went on digging her moat as if it was a lot more interesting than I was. She was wearing the same faded bathing suit. One strap slipped off her shoulder, and she pulled it back in place.

"Emma was pretty tired." I scooped up another handful of

sand. "We walked all the way to Webster's Cove and back this morning."

"Why did you go there?"

"Emma was looking for your house. She thought—"

Sissy shook her head. "I don't live in Webster's Cove."

"Where do you live, then?"

Sissy pointed in the opposite direction. "That way."

"The other day you pointed toward the Cove."

She smiled an odd little smile, more of a smirk, actually, and began to make a road to the castle with beach stones. She placed each one carefully. "Maybe I don't like unexpected company."

Maybe I don't, either, I thought. *Especially when it's you.* Out loud, I asked, "What's your last name?"

Sissy smoothed her castle's walls, stroking the sand with both hands as if it were a cat. I could see the little knobs of her spine under her skin and the sharp jut of her shoulder blades. She was definitely ignoring me—which annoyed me.

"Do you have any brothers or sisters?"

No answer.

"What's your father do?"

Still no answer.

"My dad's a math professor at the university. He—"

Sissy shrugged as if she didn't care what my father did.

I made a path with bits of broken shells and pebbles. "I'm just trying to be friendly."

"No, you're not. You're being nosy." Her face hidden by her hair, Sissy decorated her castle with bits of driftwood.

What could I say? She was right. I wasn't being friendly—I wanted to know more about her.

After a while, Sissy brushed her hair to the side and looked at me. "Emma says Dulcie's an artist. Is she good?"

I nodded. "She's getting ready for a show in Washington, D.C."

"Lucky her. I've never been there. "Sissy frowned and tossed a stone at a seagull. It missed, and the bird hopped a few feet farther away. "I've never been *anywhere*. Just here—boring Sycamore Lake, boring Webster's Cove, boring Maine."

"But Maine's beautiful. People come from all over to see the ocean and the boats and the lighthouses—"

"They must be really stupid." Sissy threw another stone, harder this time. She missed again, but the gull squawked and flew away. "I'd give anything to leave here and travel all over the world."

"Maybe when you grow up—"

"You know what? You're stupid, too."

I stared at her, but she was too busy building a little driftwood fence around her castle to look at me. "Why are you so mad all the time?" I asked her.

"What makes you think I'm mad?" She stuck a seagull's feather into the top of her castle and sat back to study the effect. "How about your mother? Is she an artist, too?"

"No."

"Why doesn't she like the lake?"

"Like Emma said, she's scared of water." I paused. Even though I didn't trust Sissy's sly eyes and mean mouth, she'd lived around here all her life. Maybe she'd heard people talk about the cottage. Unlike Erin, she wouldn't change the subject to spare my feelings.

Sissy stared at me, waiting for me to go on. Taking a deep breath, I said, "I think something happened the last summer Mom and Dulcie came to the cottage—something they don't want to talk about. Maybe something . . ." I hesitated and dropped my voice to a whisper. "Maybe something bad."

"You're right," she said. "Something bad happened, and lots of people know just what it was."

I drew in my breath and let it out slowly. "Do *you* know?"

Sissy tugged her bathing suit strap into place again and got to her feet. "That's for me to know and you to find out," she said with a smirk.

I jumped up and faced her. "You don't know anything, and neither does anyone else. You're making up stories, that's all."

"Think what you want. See if I care." Sissy turned her back on me and ran down the beach toward the Cove.

I watched her until I couldn't see her anymore. Brat. Did she really know something? Or was she lying? With one kick I demolished her castle and then splashed home through the water, sending the minnows racing for cover. The next time I saw her, I'd tell her to stay away from Emma and me.

Emma was perched on the boathouse steps, waiting for me. In the studio, Dulcie had Wagner turned up loud. I could see her through the door, painting another canvas with dark shades of purple and gray. A stormy day at the lake, I guessed.

"Where have you been?" Emma asked.

"For a walk."

"Did you see Sissy?"

I watched a gull land on one of the dock's pilings. "No," I lied.

"I wonder where she is." Emma gazed up and down the shore, as if hoping to spot Sissy.

"Oh, she'll turn up one of these days," I said, sure it was true. No matter how much I wished she'd go away, Sissy would keep coming back. She probably didn't have any other friends. Who'd want to play with someone like her?

"She'd better. Next to you, she's my best friend." Emma followed me up to the cottage, looking back every now and then, still hoping.

"Let's play a game," I said, thinking I might get her mind off Sissy. "How about Candy Land?"

"Okay." Although she didn't sound very enthusiastic, Emma watched me pull the box down from a shelf stacked with checkers, dominoes, Chinese checkers, Clue, Parcheesi, Chutes and Ladders—everything you could possibly want to play.

I laid the board on the floor between us. While Emma picked out four green playing pieces, I noticed that Mom and Dulcie had written their names in two corners of the board. The handwriting was loopy and childish, and I imagined my mom with a crayon in her hand, laboriously printing "Claire."

"What's that say?" Emma pointed to the names.

"Dulcie and Claire. I guess this was their game."

"How about this?" Emma pointed at a scribbled-over place on the third corner. "What's it say?"

Under a dark smear of black crayon, I made out the letters *T-e-r-e-s-a*. "Teresa," I whispered. "It says Teresa."

I stared at the board. A little prickle as sharp as a razor raced up my spine and tickled my scalp. *Teresa. T for Teresa.* The girl torn from the photograph, the girl I dreamed about—was her name Teresa?

"Why did somebody scribble on her name?" Emma asked.

"I don't know," I said. But I'd find out.

"Maybe Mommy didn't like her," Emma said.

"Maybe not." Suddenly uneasy, I picked up the dice. It was

weird how the cottage changed when evening shadows gathered in its corners. "Do you want to go first?"

We played three rounds, but it was hard for me to keep my mind on the silly game. My eyes returned again and again to Teresa's name. Who was she? Why was her name almost hidden by layers of black crayon? Why had she been ripped out of that photograph? I had to find out.

At the dinner table, Dulcie asked us what we'd done all afternoon. "We played Candy Land," Emma said. "I won two games, and Ali won one. She says I'm a champ." She held up her arms and flexed her muscles.

Dulcie laughed. "You've always been a champ."

Emma paused, her fork halfway to her mouth. "Who was Teresa, Mommy?"

"Teresa?" Dulcie stared at Emma, her body tense. "I don't know anyone named Teresa. Why?" She quickly got to her feet and began to gather the plates. The knives and forks rattled, the glasses clinked.

"She wrote her name on your Candy Land game." Emma followed Dulcie to the kitchen. "But somebody scribbled all over it with black crayon."

"I don't know what you're talking about." Dulcie scraped leftovers into the trash, her face hidden.

"I'll show you." Emma ran to the living room and came back with the Candy Land board. "See? Here's your name and Aunt Claire's name, and right there is Teresa's name."

Dulcie glanced at the board and shrugged. "Our mom used to buy stuff at church rummage sales. Some girl named Teresa probably owned the game before us, so we wrote our names and scribbled hers out."

It was a good explanation, but I didn't quite believe it. Something about that name upset Dulcie. She was tense, anxious.

"Remember that photo I told you about?" I asked her. "The one where the girl had been torn out? Well, her name started with *T*, and I was wondering—"

"Will you please stop talking about it? How often do I have to tell you? I don't know Teresa, I don't know why her name is on that stupid game board, and I don't know who the girl in the picture was! She could have been named Tillie or Trudy or Toni."

Dulcie's sharp voice startled both Emma and me. I stared at my aunt, puzzled. Why was she so angry?

"Don't be mad, Mommy," Emma begged, close to tears.

"I'm not mad." Dulcie plunged her hands into the soapy water and began washing the dishes with swift, jerky movements. If she weren't careful, she'd break everything in the sink.

I grabbed a dish towel. "Want me to dry?"

Keeping her back turned, Dulcie shook her head. "I'd rather you read to Emma."

"But, Mommy," Emma began.

"Go with Ali," Dulcie said. "I need some time to myself."

Emma followed me into the living room and sat beside me, her small face glum.

I put my arm around her and drew her so close I could smell the sweet scent of her hair. "Would you like to hear another chapter about the Moffats?" I asked.

Emma nodded and snuggled against me. While I read, I thought about my aunt's reaction to Emma's questions. She remembered Teresa, I was sure she did. Why wouldn't she admit it?

9

The next morning, I slept late, probably because I'd tossed and turned most of the night, dreaming about Teresa. When I stumbled downstairs, eager for orange juice, I found Emma sitting at the kitchen table with Sissy. Turning her face so only I could see it, she smiled her smirky smile.

"Look who's here!" Emma cried, obviously delighted. "Sissy came to play with me!"

"Whoop-di-do," I muttered. "Where's Dulcie?"

"In her studio. She's got lots to do today, so we shouldn't bother her."

I took my seat at the table. Dulcie had already filled a bowl with my favorite cereal. As I added milk, I was aware of Sissy sitting beside me, close enough to touch. I wasn't in the mood to put up with her. Not after a bad night's sleep.

Ignoring me, Sissy busied herself pushing Cheerios around her bowl with her spoon, sinking them into the milk and watching them pop up again. As far as I could see, she hadn't eaten any of them.

I tapped her shoulder to get her attention. "It's bad manners to play with food." Even to myself, I sounded like a crabby old lady.

"So?" Sissy shrugged and continued to stir the cereal into a gloppy mess.

"So, if Dulcie was nice enough to fix cereal for you, you should eat it."

"Dulcie didn't give me this. Emma did. I told her I wasn't hungry, but she fixed it anyway."

I looked at Emma, and she nodded. "Mommy wasn't here when Sissy came, so I got to be the hostess."

"I hate cereal unless it's got lots of sugar on it." With a frown, Sissy pushed her bowl away. "Let's go to the lake, Emmy."

"I still have my jammies on."

"Get dressed, then, slowpoke." Sissy followed us into the living room and flopped on the couch. "I'll wait here."

Leaving Sissy looking at a magazine, I took Emma to her room and helped her out of her pajamas and into her favorite yellow bathing suit.

Emma ran to the living room to make sure Sissy was still there, and I dashed upstairs and yanked on my bathing suit. When I came down, Sissy was looking at the names written on the Candy Land board. The minute she saw me, she shoved it aside. The board fell off the table and onto the floor with a faint thud.

"Candy Land is a baby's game," Sissy told me. "I outgrew it a long time ago."

"Emma likes it," I said.

"No, I don't." Emma stood in the doorway, frowning as if I'd betrayed her. "I'm way too big to play it."

"You weren't too big last night," I reminded her.

"Well, today I am!" Emma flounced past me and smiled at Sissy. "Do you want to swim or build castles?"

"Both." Sissy let Emma take her hand. I followed the two of them outside.

At the top of the steps, Sissy looked back at me. "You aren't invited."

"Sorry, but Emma doesn't go anywhere without me," I said.

"I don't need you to baby-sit me," Emma protested. She was

learning to scowl exactly like Sissy. The nasty expression didn't suit her sweet little face. Nor did the sly look she gave Sissy, hoping for her approval.

Sissy ran down the steps ahead of Emma and me and stopped at the bottom, almost as if she was afraid to go farther. "Is your mother in the studio?"

Emma nodded. "She's painting a big picture of the lake, all dark and scary, like a storm's coming." She reached for Sissy's hand. "Want to see it?"

"Dulcie'd love to meet you," I added.

Sissy took a quick look through the open door. Dulcie stood with her back to us, hard at work on another painting, darker than the first two. *Lake View Three,* she was calling this one.

"Hi, Mommy," Emma called. "We're going swimming!"

Sissy drew in her breath sharply and ducked away, as if she didn't want to be seen. Not that it mattered. Without turning around, Dulcie said, "Stay close to shore, Emma. Knee-deep, remember?"

Sissy ran to the end of the dock and posed in a diving position. Her tanned skin contrasted with her faded bathing suit and her pale hair. "Dare me?" she called to Emma.

"Not unless you swim really good," Emma said uncertainly.

"The water's over your head," I added.

"I'll do it, if you do it," Sissy said to Emma.

"No." I grabbed the straps of Emma's suit. "Emma can't swim."

"I can so!" Emma struggled to escape.

I held her tighter. "You're not allowed to jump off the dock unless your mother's here."

"Do you do everything Mommy says?" Sissy asked Emma. "Are you a little goody-goody girl?"

Emma looked confused.

"She has rules," I told Sissy, "like everyone."

"Not me," said Sissy. "I don't have any rules at all. I do whatever I want." With that, she jumped off the dock and hit the water with a big splash. She popped back up almost at once, laughing and spluttering. "Emma's a baby. She sucks her thumb and poops her pants and drinks from a bottle."

Emma began to cry. "I'm not a baby. I'm almost five years old. I can do whatever I want, too!"

With a sudden twist, Emma broke away from me and ran to the edge of the dock. Before I could stop her, she'd leapt into the lake. One second she was beside me, the next she was gone. I stared at the water in disbelief, too surprised to move.

In a few seconds, Emma's head emerged, eyes shut, mouth open, gasping for breath. Before she could sink again, I was in the lake beside her, holding her the way the lifeguard had taught me in swimming class.

Emma clung to me but turned her head to shout at Sissy, "See? I'm not a baby!"

Sissy paddled closer. Her hair floated on the water like pale yellow seaweed. "I bet you wouldn't jump if Ali wasn't here."

"I'll always be here," I told Sissy. To Emma I said, "If you do that again, I'll tell your mother."

"Tattletale, tattletale," Sissy taunted. "Nobody likes tattletales."

"I'll jump again if I want," Emma said, but she made no effort to break away from me. I had a feeling she'd scared herself. The water was deep, and she couldn't do much more than dog-paddle a few feet.

On the sand, the three of us built castles. Neither Emma nor

Sissy said a word to me. They sat close together, their heads almost touching, whispering and giggling.

"It's rude to whisper," I told Emma.

Sissy smirked. "So? Nobody invited you to play with us."

Emma carefully duplicated Sissy's smirk. "Why don't you go home? Sissy can be my babysitter."

"Two's company, three's a crowd," Sissy added. "Don't you know that yet?"

"If anyone should go home, you should!" I wanted to slap Sissy's nasty little face, but I knew that would only make things worse.

"Just ignore Ali," Sissy told Emma. "We don't like her, and we don't care what she says or what she does. She's mean."

"Meanie," Emma said. "Ali's a big fat meanie."

"Ali's so mean, Hell wouldn't want her." Sissy's eyes gleamed with malice.

Emma stared at her new friend, shocked, I think, by the word "Hell." Sissy smiled and bent over her castle, already bigger than the one she'd built yesterday. "It's not bad to say 'Hell,'" she told Emma. "It's in the Bible."

Emma glanced at me to see what I thought about this. I shook my head, but Sissy pulled Emma close and began whispering in her ear. Emma looked surprised. Then she giggled and whispered something in Sissy's ear that made her laugh.

I pulled Emma away. "What are you telling her?" I asked Sissy.

"Nothing." Sissy pressed her hands over her mouth and laughed.

"Nothing." Emma covered her mouth and laughed, too. She sounded just like Sissy.

I wanted to get up and leave, but I couldn't abandon Emma.

Instead, I moved a few feet away and watched the two of them. Their castles grew bigger and more elaborate. Everything Sissy did to hers, Emma copied. It was pathetic.

"It's nearly lunchtime," I told Emma. "Why don't we go back to the studio and get your mom?"

"Do you want to eat lunch with me?" Emma asked Sissy.

She shook her head. "It's almost time for me to go home."

"I thought you didn't have any rules," I said. "I thought you could do whatever you want."

Sissy gave me a long cold look. "Maybe I *want* to go home."

"But you don't have to go," Emma persisted. "My mommy's very nice. She fixes good peanut butter and jelly sandwiches."

Sissy made a face. "I hate peanut butter and jelly sandwiches."

"I hate them, too," Emma put in quickly. "Mommy can fix something else for us. Tuna salad, maybe."

I happened to know Emma despised tuna salad, but I didn't say anything. What was the use? She probably thought it sounded more grown up than peanut butter and jelly.

"I don't want to eat at your house." Sissy looked at me. "Not with Ali there."

"Maybe we could have a picnic, just you and me," Emma said. "Outside on the deck."

"Some other time." Sissy stood up and looked down at the castles. "They're pretty enough for a mermaid to live in," she said. "Do you like mermaids, Em?"

"I saw *The Little Mermaid* ten, twelve, a dozen times. It's my favorite movie."

Sissy tossed her head to get her hair out of her eyes. "Twelve is the same as a dozen, dummy."

"I'm not a dummy," Emma said. "I just—"

With a sudden jerk of her foot, Sissy kicked Emma's castle down.

"You ruined my castle," Emma wailed. "Now a mermaid can't live in it."

"Hey!" With a couple of kicks, I leveled Sissy's castle. "There! How do you like that?"

"I don't care." Sissy laughed. "I can build another one, better than that, and so can Emma. We have all summer to build castles for mermaids."

She laughed louder. After a moment's hesitation, Emma joined in. Shouting with laughter, they held hands and spun round and round in circles until they staggered and sprawled on the sand, still laughing.

I stared at them, slightly worried, maybe even scared of their behavior. "What's so funny?"

"Everything," Sissy giggled. "The whole stupid world is funny."

"Ali's funny." Emma laughed shrilly. "Mommy's funny. You're funny. I'm funny. The lake's funny, the seagulls are funny, the—"

Suddenly, Sissy stopped laughing. Her face turned mean. "Shut up!" she shouted at Emma. "*You* aren't funny. You're stupid. And you're a copycat."

"I'm not a copycat." Obviously bewildered by Sissy's mood change, Emma began to cry.

"Baby, baby copycat," Sissy chanted, "sat on a tack and ate a rat." Without looking back, she ran toward the Cove, still chanting.

Emma threw herself against me and pounded me with her fists. "Look what you did! You made Sissy mad! Why can't you leave us alone?"

I grabbed Emma's shoulders and held her away from me. Little as she was, her punches hurt. "I didn't do anything to that brat. She's a troublemaker, she's mean to you, she's——"

"Don't you talk like that. Sissy's my friend!"

"Some friend," I muttered. "Calling you a baby, daring you to jump off the dock, knocking your castle down. Why do you want to be friends with a girl like her?"

"You're just mad 'cause she likes me, not you."

"Don't be silly. I don't like *her*. Why should I care that she doesn't like *me*?"

"Sissy says you're jealous—that's why you don't like her, that's why you're not nice to her. You want me all to yourself!" Emma muttered.

I stared at her, amazed. "How can you believe that?"

"'Cause it's true!" Emma shouted. "Sissy doesn't lie!"

With that, she ran away from me. Surprised by the speed of her skinny little legs, I chased her. What would Dulcie think if Emma came home crying?

By the time I caught up with her, it was too late. She'd flung herself into her mother's arms.

"I hate Ali!" she sobbed. "Make her go home. I don't want a babysitter!"

Dulcie looked at me, perplexed by Emma's words. "What's going on?"

"I'll tell you later." Without waiting for my aunt or my cousin, I trudged up the steps toward the cottage.

If Dulcie wanted to send me home, fine. Sissy had turned Emma into a nasty little brat, just like herself, and I was sick of both of them.

10

Dulcie fixed the usual peanut butter and jelly sandwiches and chocolate milk for lunch.

Emma pushed her plate away. "I don't like peanut butter and jelly," she whined.

Dulcie looked at her in surprise. "Since when?"

"Since now." Out went Emma's lower lip in a classic pout. "They're for babies."

"What do you mean? Ali and I eat them. We're not babies."

"I want cheese," Emma said.

"I thought you liked tuna salad," I said.

Emma glared at me. "I can like whatever I like!"

Dulcie put her hands over mine and Emma's. "Would you girls please tell me what's going on?"

"It's Sissy's fault," I told her. "She's a bad influence on Emma."

"She is not!" Emma scowled at me.

"Then why was she so nasty to you?" I asked, trying to stay calm.

"She wasn't," Emma said. "*You* were!"

I stared at my cousin, truly shocked. "What did *I* do?"

Emma turned to her mother tearfully. "Ali called me stupid and said I was a baby."

"I did not!" I told Dulcie. "I'd never say anything like that. Sissy called her names, not me."

Emma climbed into her mother's lap and began to cry. "Ali's not nice to me and Sissy," she insisted. "Just 'cause she's bigger, she thinks she's the boss."

Dulcie rocked Emma, but her eyes were on me. I had a sick feeling that my aunt wasn't sure which one of us to believe. From her mother's lap, Emma watched me closely, her face almost as mean as Sissy's.

"It's not true," I said weakly. "Sissy—"

"Ali pushed me off the dock, too," Emma interrupted. "If Sissy hadn't been there, I would have drowned—"

"That's a lie and you know it, Emma!" Close to tears I turned to Dulcie. "Sissy dared Emma to jump. I tried to stop her, but she got away from me. She wants to do everything Sissy does."

Dulcie looked from Emma to me and back to Emma, her eyes worried. "I can't believe Ali would push you off the dock, Emma."

"Yes, she would," Emma insisted. "Ali's so bad, even Hell doesn't want her."

"Emma!" Dulcie stared at her daughter. "Where did you pick up that kind of talk?"

I spoke before Emma had a chance to answer. "Sissy told her cussing was fine. She could say whatever she wanted."

Dulcie stood Emma on the floor and got to her feet. "I've heard enough. Sit down and eat your sandwich."

"I don't want any stinky lunch!" Emma started to run out of the kitchen, but Dulcie grabbed her arm and stopped her. "What's gotten into you?" she asked. "You've never acted like this before. Never."

"I told you," I said. "It's Sissy's fault."

Dulcie ignored me. This was between her and Emma. "Sit down," she said. "And eat your lunch."

Emma took her place between Dulcie and me. She didn't look at either of us but ate quietly, her head down, her jaws working as she chewed. She left half the sandwich on her plate, despite Dulcie's pleas to eat it all.

"Do you want me to read a Moffat story?" I asked, hoping to resume our normal relationship.

Emma scowled. "I hate the Moffats. They're dumb. Just like you!"

"Don't talk to Ali like that," Dulcie said. "We never call anyone dumb."

"Leave me alone," Emma said. "You're dumb, too."

Dulcie frowned. "If this is how you act when Sissy comes here, I don't want you to play with her anymore."

Emma responded with a major temper tantrum. She screamed and cried. She told Dulcie she hated her. She threw herself on the floor and kicked.

Finally, Dulcie hauled Emma to her room and put her to bed. Closing the door firmly, she left her to cry herself to sleep.

She dropped back into her chair, her face puzzled. "How can this child have so much influence on Emma so quickly?"

I'd been wondering about this myself. "Maybe it's because Emma's never had a friend before. She wants Sissy to like her, so she does everything Sissy tells her to do."

Dulcie went to the stove and poured herself another cup of coffee. With her back to me, she said, "I guess I really don't know much about kids. Sometimes I wonder if I was ever actually one myself."

She laughed, not as if it was funny, more as if it was sad or odd. "I have friends who remember every detail of their childhoods, their teachers' names, what they wore to someone's birthday party when they were eight years old, what they got for

Christmas when they were ten. Me—I can't remember a thing before my teen years."

Dulcie carried her coffee outside. The way she let the screen door slam shut behind her hinted she wasn't expecting me to follow. She sat at the picnic table, her back to the window, her shoulders hunched. Even without seeing her face, I knew she was unhappy. Maybe her summer wasn't going any better than mine. Who could have imagined a kid like Sissy would turn up and spoil everything?

I stretched out on the sofa with *To Kill a Mockingbird*. I was on the seventh chapter with many more to go.

While I read, I heard a car approaching the cottage. I sat up and looked out the window. For some reason I expected to see Mom and Dad, but a big red Jeep emerged from the woods. Dulcie walked toward it hesitantly, apparently unsure who it was.

"Dulcie, it *is* you!" A plump woman with short silvery blond hair jumped out of the Jeep and stood there grinning as Dulcie approached. Her tailored shorts and pink polo shirt contrasted sharply with my aunt's black T-shirt and paint-spattered jeans.

She stopped just short of giving Dulcie a hug. "Look at you," she exclaimed, "you're just as skinny as ever!"

"I'm sorry," Dulcie said, smoothing her mop of uncombed curls back from her face, "but I don't remember—"

"Well, no wonder. I wasn't this fat when we were kids!" She laughed. "I'm Jeanine Reynolds—Donaldson now. We used to play together when you and Claire came to the lake."

"Jeanine," Dulcie repeated. "Jeanine. . . . I'm afraid I—"

"Oh, don't worry about it. Good grief, it's been what? Thirty years, I guess."

"My sister would probably remember you."

"Is Claire here, too?"

"No, but her daughter, Ali, is staying with us this summer."

Jeanine nodded and looked at the cottage. "It's just the same as I remember. I hear you had Joe Russell working on it. He's good. Not cheap, though."

"Compared to New York, he's a bargain," Dulcie said.

Jeanine sat down at the picnic table. "Is that where you live?"

Dulcie nodded. "Would you like something to drink? I've got mint tea in the fridge, if you'd like that."

"Anything, as long as it's cold," Jeanine said. "Today's a real scorcher."

Leaving the woman on the deck, Dulcie came inside. By then I was in the kitchen, ready to help with cheese and crackers if she wanted them.

Dulcie rolled her eyes. "There goes the afternoon," she whispered.

A few minutes later, I was setting down a tray with an assortment of crackers, cheese, and sliced fruit. Dulcie poured glasses of iced tea for herself and Jeanine and offered me a can of soda. The three of us settled ourselves comfortably under the patio umbrella.

"My daughter, Erin, tells me you're an artist," Jeanine said. "I'm not surprised. When we were kids, you were always drawing. You carried a sketchbook and pencils everywhere we went."

Dulcie smiled as if she were beginning to warm up to Jeanine. "Yes, I guess I did."

"You were so talented. We were always asking you to draw pictures for us. Teresa, especially. She was crazy about your mermaids—remember?"

All traces of friendliness suddenly disappeared from my aunt's face. She gripped her glass of iced tea and shook her head. "No, I don't remember Teresa. Or any mermaids I might have drawn."

I held my breath and waited to hear what Jeanine would say next.

Staring at Dulcie in disbelief, she said, "You *can't* have forgotten Teresa. What happened to her has haunted me all my life——"

"I don't know what you're talking about." Dulcie stood up so fast her chair fell over with a bang that made both Jeanine and me jump. Her hair seemed wilder than before, and her body was so tense, you could have snapped her in two.

She stood there a moment, glass in hand, avoiding our eyes. "Excuse me," she said in a lower voice. "I have work to do, paintings to finish for a show this fall."

Without looking at us, Dulcie left Jeanine and me sitting at the picnic table and ran down to her studio, her sandals flapping on the steps. The door slammed. For a few seconds after that, the only sound was the lake quietly rippling against the shore.

"Oh, dear." Jeanine's face flushed. "I guess I shouldn't have come, but I—well, I've always wondered what became of Claire and Dulcie. I thought——"

She broke off and reached for her car keys. "I'm so sorry, Ali. I never meant to upset your aunt. I hope she, you— Oh, I just don't know why I'm so thoughtless, coming here, bringing up the past." She started to rise from her chair.

I touched her hand to keep her from leaving. "Please tell me what you're talking about. Who was Teresa? What happened to her?"

Jeanine sipped her iced tea silently, her eyes on the horizon and the blue sky beyond. She wanted to finish what she'd started, I could tell.

Sure enough, the next thing she said was, "I don't see how Dulcie could have forgotten that child—or even me, for that matter. The two of us spent a lot of time at this cottage, especially

Teresa. Why, your grandmother used to call us her borrowed daughters."

She paused to watch a squirrel dart across the deck and leap onto a pine tree. A branch swayed, and he was gone. Her eyes turned back to me. "Your mother didn't tell you about Teresa?"

I toyed with my empty soda can, turning it this way and that. "Mom never talks about the lake. She hates it so much, she almost didn't let me come with Dulcie." I hesitated and rubbed the wet ring my soda can had made on the table. "You saw how Dulcie is—she claims she doesn't remember anything. But—" I stopped, not sure what to tell Jeanine. Her face was kind, her eyes understanding, and I desperately wanted to talk to someone about Teresa.

"But what?" Jeanine helped herself to another slice of cheese.

I watched her sandwich the cheese between two crackers. "Well, before Dulcie invited me here, I found an old photo of her and Mom when they were kids. Another girl had been sitting beside Dulcie, but someone had torn her out of the picture. On the back, all that was left of her name was a *T*. Mom got really upset and swore she didn't know anyone whose name started with *T*."

"And you think it was Teresa," Jeanine said.

"The lake was in the background, so it *must* have been her."

Jeanine nodded and helped herself to another piece of cheese. She seemed to be waiting for me to tell her more.

"Last night, I got out an old Candy Land game," I went on. "Mom and Dulcie had written their names on the board. Teresa's name was there, too. But someone had scribbled over it with a black crayon. Dulcie said she didn't know why 'Teresa' was written on the board. She got mad and shouted at me."

I lowered my head, almost ashamed to finish. "Dulcie remembers Teresa—I'm sure she does. Why would she lie about it?"

"Maybe it has something to do with Teresa's death." As she spoke, Jeanine looked at the lake, her face expressionless.

"Teresa *died?*" Shocked, I gripped the soda can and stared at Jeanine. I'd never imagined Teresa dead. All this time, I'd pictured her living around here somewhere, stopping by for a visit, forcing Dulcie to remember her. "How did she die?"

"It was the last summer your mother and aunt came to the lake." Jeanine sipped her tea. "For some reason, no one knows why, Teresa went out in your grandfather's canoe all by herself. It was rainy, foggy. The canoe washed up nearby, but . . ."

Shivers raced up and down my bare arms.

Jeanine looked at me, and a shadow crossed her face—worry, maybe. "I hope I haven't upset you." She patted my hand, white knuckled from its grip on the soda can. "Teresa's been gone a long time now."

She broke a cracker into pieces and tossed the crumbs to a pair of sparrows hopping around our feet. For a moment, she sat silently, watching the birds fight over the crumbs. Without looking at me, she said, "It must have been very painful for Claire and Dulcie. It certainly was for me."

She threw more crumbs to the sparrows. Several others arrived, as if word had gotten out that food was available.

"What was Teresa like?" I asked at last.

"Just an ordinary kid, I guess. Smart, kind of cute, but . . ." While Jeanine talked, her eyes drifted from the sparrows to the bumblebees droning in the hollyhocks.

"But what?"

"Oh, nothing. I'm just running my mouth, as usual." She looked at her watch. "My goodness, it's almost time for supper, and I haven't got a thing in the house. I'd better go."

Jumping to her feet, Jeanine gave me a quick hug. "Please don't worry about what I told you. It happened so long ago. Maybe your aunt and your mother really have forgotten. After all, they didn't spend the rest of their lives here, listening to people talk about poor Teresa."

After landing a kiss on my cheek, Jeanine hurried to the Jeep. "Tell Dulcie I'd love to see her again," she called, ". . . if she wants to see me."

With a smile and a wave, she put the Jeep in reverse and backed down the drive.

Long after Jeanine left, I sat on the deck, gazing out at the lake's calm water. No wonder Mom hadn't wanted me, her one and only child, to spend the summer here. No wonder she was scared of water and boats. No wonder she feared for my safety. If Teresa could drown, so could I.

But I had a feeling there was more to Teresa's death—much more. Jeanine hadn't told me all she knew. She'd been edgy, nervous, uneasy. While she'd talked, she'd looked at everything but me: the lake, the sparrows, the bumblebees in the hollyhocks. And she'd left in a hurry, before I'd had a chance to ask her any more questions.

It seemed the answer to one question always led to another question. And that answer to another question, and so on and so on. Was anything ever settled and done with?

⟞꙰11꙰⟝

I was still sitting on the deck, half asleep in the afternoon sun, when I heard Emma's bare feet patter into the kitchen. The refrigerator door opened and shut. Soon she was staring at me from the doorway. A purple Popsicle dripped down her arm and stained her mouth.

"You can't make Sissy go away," Emma said. "She'll be my friend forever, no matter what." Her face was closed off and hostile.

Grumpy and out of sorts from the heat, I frowned at Emma. "Your mother doesn't want you to play with Sissy anymore."

Emma sucked her Popsicle, leaching the purple out, something I'd enjoyed doing when I was her age. "Mommy can't make Sissy go away. No one can."

I picked up a *New Yorker* magazine and fanned myself. I was tired of the conversation, if you could call it that. "Do you want to go swimming?"

Emma studied the colorless lump of ice on the Popsicle stick. "With you?"

"I don't see anyone else. Do you?"

"Not now." Emma scowled at me. "But I bet we'll see Sissy later." With that, she stalked off to her room. I followed to see if she needed help with her bathing suit.

"I can do it myself," she said and closed the door in my face.

A few minutes later, the two us were wading in the shallow

water along the shore. To my relief—and Emma's disappointment—Sissy wasn't in sight. The ruined castles lay where we'd left them. Emma knelt beside hers and began to repair it.

Leaving my pouty little cousin to work on her castle, I began collecting interesting stones and driftwood. I hadn't talked to Dulcie about my idea yet, but I was sure she'd let me use her potter's wheel.

After a while, Emma came over and nudged my pile of stones with her toe. "Want to play in the water?"

I took her hand, and we waded into the lake. Emma seemed almost herself. She splashed and dog-paddled in the shallow water, wallowing like a puppy.

When I noticed her lips and nails turning blue, I led her to shore and dried her with a big beach towel.

"Do you want to go back to the cottage?" I asked. "You're shivering."

Emma shook her head. Droplets of water flew from her wet hair. She spread the towel on a sunny patch of sand and sat on it. I saw her glance toward the Cove as if hoping to see Sissy.

"Why did Sissy get mad at me?" Emma asked. "We were having fun and laughing, and then all of a sudden she got mad."

I wasn't sure what to say. If I criticized Sissy, Emma would get cranky again. To avoid that, I shrugged and said I didn't know why Sissy acted the way she did. "Some kids are like that."

Emma hung her head and toyed with strands of her wet hair. "Sissy mixes me up," she whispered. "Sometimes she's nice, and other times she's mean."

"Maybe we should go to the Cove tomorrow," I said, "and find some other kids for you to play with."

Emma hunched her bony shoulders. "I don't want any friend but Sissy."

I lifted her chin so I could see her face. "You just admitted she's mean. Why do you like her so much?"

Emma pulled away, pouty again. "I wished and wished for a friend, and she came."

I looked at her more closely. "Wishing didn't have anything to do with it. You were at the beach, and she was there at the same time. That's how people meet."

Emma poked at the sand with a stick. "She came because I wanted her to come."

"That's what you think." Sissy stood a few feet away, her hands on her hips, her hair a cottony tangle. "Nobody can make me do anything. I only do what *I* want to do."

"Where did *you* come from?" I was definitely not happy to see her.

Sissy pointed toward the woods behind us. "I sneaked up on you, didn't I? I'm as quiet as an Indian."

All smiles, Emma jumped to her feet and ran to grab Sissy's hand. "I was scared you were mad at me."

Pulling her hand away, Sissy flopped down beside me. "How old are you?"

"Thirteen. Why?"

"Do you have a boyfriend?"

"No."

"When my sister was thirteen, she had a boyfriend." Sissy looked me over, taking in my skinny legs and arms. "She had a really good figure, and she wore lipstick and nail polish. She was pretty, too. In fact, she won a beauty contest when she was only fifteen—Miss Webster's Cove. She got to ride in a motorboat parade and throw roses in the water." Sissy hugged her knees to her chest as if she was holding tight to the memory.

"I didn't know you had a sister." Emma squeezed in between Sissy and me. "Why doesn't she ever come here with you?"

Sissy picked up a small scallop shell and examined it. "She's grown up now. Why would she want to hang out with kids?"

"What's her name?" Emma asked. "How old is she? Is she still Miss Webster's Cove?"

"Don't you know it's rude to ask so many questions?" Tossing the shell away, Sissy jumped to her feet and pointed at the lake. "Look at those guys out there."

Not far from shore, two boys sped toward us in a motorboat, towing a suntanned girl on water skis. Over the engine's noise, we heard them laughing and shouting to each other.

"Lucky ducks," Sissy said. "I wish I had a boyfriend with a boat." Her voice was so full of longing, I almost felt sorry for her.

"You're too young to have a boyfriend," I said. "Just wait till you're a teenager. You'll have plenty of boys to take you water-skiing."

"Don't be stupid." Sissy pulled at a strand of hair, her face angry. "I'll never have a boyfriend."

"Why do you care?" Emma said. "Boys are dumb."

Sissy gave her a look intended to wither. "What do *you* know about boys?"

Emma drew in her breath and edged away from Sissy. She wasn't about to argue.

"I'm hot," Sissy said. "Let's go swimming."

Emma jumped up and splashed into the lake behind Sissy. I followed, letting the cold water creep up my legs, chilling my skin. When she was waist deep, Sissy dove in and disappeared.

A few seconds later she popped out of the water and ducked Emma. The moment Emma came up for air, Sissy ducked her again. And again. And again. Her face was angry, her eyes cruel.

By the time I pulled Emma away, she was spluttering and coughing.

"What were you doing?" I shouted at Sissy. "You could drown somebody that way!"

Sissy paddled a few feet away, her anger replaced with a sly grin. "I was just fooling around," she said. "Don't get so worked up."

"You scared Emma."

"Can't you two take a joke?"

"It wasn't funny!" I yelled.

Emma clung to me, shivering and crying. "I want to go home!" she wailed.

"That's just where we're going." I stalked back to shore, carrying Emma. "You go home, too, Sissy. And don't come back till you can be nice."

Sissy stayed where she was, knee-deep in the lake, a skinny kid in a faded bathing suit. "I was playing," she yelled after us. "That's all. It was a game."

I guessed that was the closest to an apology we'd ever hear from Sissy. But I was still mad. And Emma was still upset.

"Never do that again!" I shouted.

With a smirk, Sissy spread her hands, palms out, and sloshed to shore. Turning toward the Cove, she walked away.

For once, Emma wasn't sorry to see her go.

The next morning was bright and sunny, a perfect day—too pretty to work, Dulcie said. Instead of going to the studio, she loaded Emma and me into the car and headed for the ocean. We explored the rocky cliffs and the lighthouse at Pemaquid Point, and threw bread crumbs to the seagulls like all the other tourists. We stopped in Boothbay and browsed in art galleries and craft shops. I bought two Maine T-shirts, one for me and one for my friend Staci. Dulcie treated Emma to a fuzzy handmade bear, a notebook with a hand-tooled leather cover for me, and warm wool sweaters for all three of us. On the way home, we stuffed ourselves at a fudge factory.

The next day was just as perfect as the day before. Dulcie took us to a dairy farm, where we bought slabs of pale cheese and jars of honey and blueberry preserves. We spent the afternoon riding rented horses on wooded trails.

The sunshine came to an end with an evening thunderstorm. A heavy rain fell all night and into the next morning. At breakfast, Dulcie frowned at the gray skies. "Back to work," she said glumly.

Just as Emma and I began a game of Candy Land, we heard what sounded like a scream or a shout of some kind.

"What was that?" Emma whispered.

"I don't know." I went to the door and peered out into the rain, my heart thumping with fear. Had it been a cry for help? Someone drowning?

Dulcie came running toward me, her hair wild from the wind and the rain. Her wet, paint-smeared T-shirt clung to her skinny frame, and her faded jeans dripped water.

"It's your mother," I told Emma. "Something's wrong."

Emma knocked the board aside, scattering the playing pieces, and ran outside. I followed her, unable to imagine what had happened, and stared at my aunt fearfully. I'd never seen her cry, never seen her so upset.

"My paintings," Dulcie wailed. "Someone broke into the

studio and wrecked everything. All my work, my paints, my brushes."

Emma clung to her mother. "Mommy, Mommy," she sobbed. "Don't cry."

"I can't believe it," I whispered. "Who would do something like that?"

"Come and look." Dulcie ran back down the stairs to the studio.

Emma and I hurried after her. The rain pelted us, and we held tightly to the railing, afraid of slipping on the wet steps.

From the studio's doorway, Dulcie gestured at the wreckage. It looked as if someone had thrown bucketsful of sand and lake water on the floor. Paint tubes were scattered, tops off, colors oozing out. Brushes stiff with dried paint littered the worktable. Splattered with ugly shades of reds, yellows, and green, the paintings lay in a heap in a corner.

One painting leaned against the easel. In black paint and large clumsy letters, someone had scrawled:

I'M WATCHING YOU
TELL THE TRUTH
OR ELSE

Emma clutched her mother's hand and pointed at the painting. "Bones," she whispered. "There's bones at the bottom."

I drew in my breath. She was right. In the painting's lower right-hand corner, in the darkest part, was a small, clumsily drawn skeleton.

Hiding her face, Emma cried, "I don't want to see the bones."

I didn't want to see them, either. As scared as Emma, I looked at Dulcie. "Do you think it's—" I broke off, afraid to say Teresa's name. The damp air was full of her, she was everywhere, I could almost feel her cold hands touching my shoulders.

In a fury, Dulcie pulled away from Emma and grabbed a tube of black paint. She squeezed what was left of it on the painting, spreading it with her hands until she'd covered the words and the bones. "There—it's gone!"

"But—"

Dulcie turned on me. "I don't want to hear another word about this. It's a case of teenage vandalism—that's all." She picked up a broom. "Now, if you don't mind, I want to clean up."

I backed away, hurt by the anger in her voice. "Can't I help?"

"Take Emma to the cottage, read to her, play games, do what I hired you to do." Dulcie gripped the broom so tightly her knuckles whitened. The veins in her neck stood out like knotted cords, and she was shaking. "I'll take care of this."

I reached for Emma's hand, but she clung to Dulcie. "I want to stay with you, Mommy. Let me help you."

"You heard what I said. Go with Ali and leave me alone." Dulcie freed herself from Emma and began sweeping the sand toward the door. Underneath her mop of wild hair, her face was an odd colorless shade—ashen, I guess, like people in shock.

Emma began to cry, but Dulcie was in no mood to sympathize. "Please, Ali, take her to the cottage."

Somehow I managed to haul Emma up the steps, rain and wind and all, and get her inside.

"Mommy's mad at me," Emma sobbed. "She hates me."

"No, Em, she's not mad, just upset." Trying to comfort her, I began stripping her wet clothes off, not easy when your hands are shaking. Dulcie's anger had frightened me. I'd never seen her behave like that. But the words and the skeleton scribbled on the painting had scared me even more.

As I rubbed Emma dry with a big soft towel, I stared out the window. All I saw was rain. All I heard was the wind in the pines and the monotonous lapping of lake water. I shivered, suddenly sure something was out there, hidden in the trees, watching us.

I helped Emma into a T-shirt and fastened her overall buckles. Warm and dry, she was still shivering. After I changed my clothes, I fixed cookies and hot chocolate. Then I read all three *Lonely Doll* stories, trying to comfort myself as well as Emma.

By the time we settled down to play Candy Land, we were both feeling pretty normal. Maybe Dulcie was right. The boys we'd seen in the motorboat could have vandalized the studio.

But why had they left that message? What did they think Dulcie was lying about? Why did they draw bones on her painting? It didn't make sense.

Let Dulcie believe what she wanted, especially if it made her feel better, but those boys hadn't vandalized her studio. Someone else had.

Emma shook the dice and made her green man hop along the road to Candy Land. "Your turn, Ali."

I shook the dice and moved my blue man seven steps closer to the corner where Teresa had written her name.

What really happened the day Teresa drowned?

~✺12✺~

A sudden rattling sound at the front door startled me. I wasn't sure what I expected to see, but for once I was almost glad it was Sissy. Nose pressed against the screen, she yanked at the door, hooked tight against the wind. "Let me in!"

Emma went to the door. Without opening it, she frowned at Sissy. "You can't come in unless you promise to be nice."

"I *told* you I was just fooling around," Sissy said. "You have to learn to take a little teasing."

"But—"

"Can I come in or not?"

Emma reached up and slowly unhooked the door. "If you're mean, you have to go home."

Good for you, Emma, I thought.

"You're all wet," Emma said.

"It's raining," Sissy said. "Or didn't you notice?"

"Aren't you cold?" I asked.

Sissy shook her head. Her wet hair swung, spraying water like a dog shaking itself.

"But all you have on is a bathing suit."

"So? You wear a bathing suit to go in the water. What difference does it make if you get it wet in the rain or in the lake?" Sissy's voice dripped sarcasm, just as her hair dripped water, but her teeth chattered as she spoke, and her lips were blue with cold.

I grabbed a towel from the bathroom and handed it to her. "Dry yourself off. You're dripping all over the floor."

"Do you want a sweatshirt?" Emma asked.

Sissy shrugged. Taking that as a yes, Emma ran to her room and returned with a bright yellow Winnie the Pooh sweatshirt.

"I'm not wearing that," Sissy said. "I hate yellow, and I hate Pooh."

"I do, too," Emma said quickly, even though I knew it was her favorite sweatshirt, my birthday present to her last year.

"Then why do you think I want to wear it?" Sissy asked.

Poor Emma was in over her head, and she knew it. Shoulders drooping, she walked back to her room, dragging the sweatshirt behind her.

"That wasn't very nice," I told Sissy. "Maybe you should go home—like Emma told you."

Without answering, Sissy did a little dance around the living room. She turned and spun, hair and towel flying, then collapsed on the couch.

"I used to have this book." Sissy picked up *The Lonely Doll* and leafed through it, pausing now and then to look at an illustration. "Where do you think Edith's parents are? Does she live all by herself?"

"I don't know. It never says."

"It's kind of strange, don't you think? A little girl living alone, and then these bears come along, and Mr. Bear's like her father and Little Bear's like her brother, but there's still no mother."

Sissy waited to hear my opinion. "I never really thought about it," I admitted.

"It bothered me when I was little," Sissy said quietly. "But now it's just another silly kid story." She tossed the book aside and looked around the living room. "Where's the TV?"

"We don't have one. My aunt hates TV. She says it rots your mind."

"She sure has some stupid ideas." Sissy slid down lower on the couch, stretching her skinny legs way out in front of her. "I don't have a TV, either. I was really hoping you did."

I felt a little twinge of hope. Maybe she would stop coming around now that she knew there was no TV to watch. "I'm going to see if Emma's okay," I said.

"She's one spoiled kiddo," Sissy said.

"It takes one to know one," I muttered under my breath.

I found Emma in her room, surrounded by heaps of clothing she'd pulled out of her bureau. Holding up a faded red sweat-shirt, she said, "Do you think Sissy will like this? It even has a hood."

"Oh, Emma," I sighed. "Stop trying to please her. She promised to be nice, remember? And now she's being her usual horrible self."

Ignoring me, Emma ran down the hall to the living room. "How's this, Sissy? It used to be Mommy's. It's too big for me, but I bet it's just right for you."

Sissy took the sweatshirt and slipped it over her head. "It's kind of ugly, but at least it's not yellow."

"Want to play a different game? We have Clue and checkers and Parcheesi and—"

"I'm bored by board games." Sissy laughed. "Get it? Bored and board?"

Emma laughed to please Sissy, but I don't think she understood the joke. Not that it was very funny. I didn't even bother to smile.

"Where's your mother?" Sissy asked Emma.

"She's in her studio." Emma frowned. "Some bad teenagers

wrecked it last night. They ruined all her paintings, and Mommy got mad."

Sissy glanced at me and smoothed her damp hair behind her ears. "It was probably kids from Union Mills. They're always doing stuff like that. My sister dated a boy from there, but Daddy chased him off. He was no-good white trash, Daddy said."

For a second, a look of sadness crossed Sissy's face, but it was gone so fast, I wasn't sure if I'd really seen it.

Emma nodded as if she knew all about the no-good white trash in Union Mills, but Sissy leaned toward me, her cold eyes fixed on mine. "Did Dulcie call the cops?"

I shook my head. "Not yet."

"It would be a waste of time. They'd never figure out who did it. If you want to know the truth, the cops in this town are morons."

I slid away from her, tired of her know-it-all attitude about everything. "What makes you think you know anything about the police?"

"Just listen to this." Sissy scooted toward me, closing the gap between us. "Did Dulcie ever tell you about Teresa?"

"The girl who drowned in the lake?"

Emma stared at me. "Teresa's dead?"

"That's what usually happens when you drown," Sissy said, laughing again at her own joke.

I'd forgotten Emma didn't know, but it was too late to take the words back. "It was a long time ago," I told her, "way back when your mom and my mom were little."

"Poor Teresa, poor, poor Teresa." Emma shuddered and moved closer to me.

I put an arm around her. "It's very sad," I whispered to her, "but don't cry, please don't."

Emma sniffed and wiped her eyes with her hands. With one finger, she touched Teresa's name on the game board. "She wrote this," she told Sissy. "She played here before . . . before she . . ."

"Before she *died*," Sissy finished Emma's sentence. Turning to me, she said, "You know what else? The cops never found Teresa's body. *That's* how dumb they are. Teresa's parents couldn't even bury her!"

Emma pressed her face against my side and covered her ears. Almost as shocked as Emma, I hugged my cousin and stared wordlessly at Sissy.

She sat back, enjoying the effect of her story. "Poor old Teresa. Her bones are still out there someplace, deep down in the dark, dark water. All cold and lonely."

"Is Teresa a ghost?" Emma asked in a shaky voice. "Do her bones come out?"

"Maybe." Sissy kept grinning. "Maybe not. Who knows?"

The room seemed to grow cold and damp and shadowy, and I held Emma tighter. I knew I should tell Sissy to shut up and go home, but I didn't. Jeanine hadn't said Teresa's body was still in the lake. Maybe she'd left that out because she didn't want to scare me. What else had she kept to herself?

Sissy pushed herself even nearer to me and grinned. Her face was so close I could see the cavities in her small yellow teeth. "Want to hear the best part?"

Ignoring Emma's whimper, I nodded, as eager to hear as she was eager to tell.

"Everybody thinks your mothers were with Teresa the day she drowned," Sissy said. "After all, she fell out of your grandfather's canoe. What was she doing taking it out all by herself?"

"Make her stop," Emma whispered to me. "I don't want to hear any more."

"It's okay," I told her, my eyes held fast by Sissy's. "You can go to your room if you don't want to hear."

Emma shook her head and again hid her face against my side.

"Teresa's mother told the police to talk to your mothers," Sissy went on. "But the cops were too dumb to get anything out of them."

She paused a second. "Some people say Dulcie pushed Teresa into the water, and then she and your mother left her there to drown—that the canoe washed up on some rocks, and they walked home and lied and lied and lied. They said they'd never been out of the cottage, they hadn't seen Teresa, they didn't know why she took the canoe. *That's* why they never came back here—they were scared of what they'd done."

While she'd been talking, Sissy's voice had risen higher and higher. Shaking with anger, she paused and took a deep breath, then another, and another, her chest heaving under the sweatshirt.

"Your mothers should be punished for what they did to Teresa," she said in a calm voice. "Murder—that's what they did. *Murder.*"

"How do you know all this?" I felt cold, achy, weak in the knees, as if I was coming down with the flu. Or maybe something worse—fatal, even. If Sissy meant to scare Emma and me, she'd done it.

"People still talk about Teresa," Sissy said with a shrug. "Unlike your mothers, nobody in Webster's Cove has forgotten her."

Turning to Emma, Sissy pulled her hands away from her ears and whispered, "Oh, and lots of people have seen Teresa's ghost. On foggy days, they hear her calling, *'Help, help, don't let Dulcie drown me.'*"

Emma covered her ears again and started rocking back and forth, humming loudly to keep from hearing.

I shoved Sissy away from Emma. "Shut up!" I yelled. "Shut up! It's not true, you liar." I raised my hand to slap her face, but she spun out of my reach, laughing.

"Teenagers didn't wreck Dulcie's paintings," Sissy crowed. "Teresa did. She's still here. You know it, and so does Dulcie."

"No," Emma wailed, "no!"

"Teresa could be *anywhere*," Sissy went on. "She could be in this room right this minute, hiding in the shadows, just waiting to drown you like your mom drowned her. She could come through the window and get you in the middle of the night, she could—"

"Get out of this house, Sissy!" I rushed at her again, wanting to hit her hard, to hurt her, to make her admit it was all a lie.

"I'm going, I'm going." Pulling the hood of the red sweatshirt over her hair, Sissy stuck out her tongue and ran into the rain. "Watch out for Teresa!"

Emma hurled herself into my arms. "Teresa can't get me, she can't drown me. Not unless I go to the lake where her bones are. And I'll never go there again."

I hugged her shivering body. "Sissy made it all up," I murmured into her ear. "The next time she comes over, we'll tell her to go away. We won't let her in."

Emma cried herself to sleep in my lap. Sissy had exhausted her. She'd exhausted me, too, but I was too upset to sleep. I wanted to believe what I'd told Emma. It was a lie, all a lie. Our mothers had told the truth, they hadn't been in the canoe that day. Teresa was dead and gone—she wasn't in the house, she hadn't wrecked the studio.

But no matter how hard I argued with myself, I had a feeling that at least some of what Sissy had said was true. Hadn't I dreamt about Teresa night after night? Didn't ghosts come to people in dreams and demand justice? *Tell the truth,* the note had said. *Tell the truth or else.*

Or else what?

Emma stirred and woke up. "I want Mommy," she said sleepily.

As she slid off my lap, I peered into her eyes. "I know Sissy scared you, Em, but don't tell your mother what she said."

Emma looked puzzled. "But—"

"Please promise you won't tell." I held her tightly to keep her from running down to the studio. "Dulcie doesn't want to hear anything about Teresa. You should have seen her face when Jeanine Donaldson started talking about her. She was so upset, she walked off."

"But suppose the ghost gets in our house? Suppose it's . . . already here?" Emma peered fearfully at the familiar living room. Her eyes lingered on shadowy corners.

"Teresa's not here." I tried to sound sure, but it was all too easy to picture Teresa watching us from the hall, perched on the steps, maybe, or here in the living room, hovering near the Candy Land board where she'd once written her name. As Sissy had said, she could be anywhere.

"She got in the studio," Emma whispered. "She drew the bones. Mommy should know she was there. Teresa might hurt her."

"Teresa can't hurt anyone. She's—" I stopped myself from saying "dead." Gripping Emma's shoulders so tightly she winced, I said, "Promise not to tell."

When I released her, Emma relaxed her shoulders and let her head slump. Without looking at me, she muttered, "Okay."

I pulled her hands from behind her back before she had time to uncross her fingers. "That's cheating, Em. Promise again."

In a low voice, Emma said, "Are you sure Teresa won't get us?"

"I'm positive," I lied. At this point, I had no idea what Teresa might do. Maybe she was real, maybe she wasn't. Maybe she wanted to hurt Dulcie, maybe she wanted to hurt Emma and me, maybe she was just drifting around in the rain and the mist. It was hard to look at my cousin and pretend I wasn't just as scared as she was.

Emma's eyes welled with tears, but she drew her finger back and forth across her heart. "I promise not to tell Mommy." Her voice was so low I could barely hear her.

Hoping I could trust her, I gave her a hug. Then, making an effort to speak in a normal voice, I asked, "Would you like a glass of juice? And a chocolate-chip cookie?"

Emma followed me to the kitchen and sat at the counter while I fixed our snack. She took a small bite of the cookie and a tiny sip of juice. Then she pushed both away. "Not hungry," she mumbled.

I toyed with my cookie, no hungrier than Emma. Outside the leaves rustled, and I shivered. *Go away, Teresa, go away. Leave us alone.*

—❧13❧—

The next morning, the rain stopped, but the mist hung on. I was beginning to think Mom hadn't exaggerated the lake's bad weather. Or the hordes of mosquitoes and gnats that seemed immune to bug sprays.

When I came downstairs, I saw Dulcie staring out the window at the water. After a while, she said, "I'd better get back to work."

She'd cleaned up most of the mess and discovered that the paintings weren't as badly damaged as she'd thought. Except for the one she'd smeared with black paint, she'd managed to clean them.

After she left, I sat at the table and enjoyed a cup of coffee with plenty of sugar and cream. Mom never let me drink it at home, but Dulcie said caffeine wouldn't hurt me. She lived on it herself. Emma was still sleeping—she'd been awake all night with bad dreams, but she wouldn't tell Dulcie what they were about. I was pretty sure Sissy's story had inspired her nightmares. I'd dreamed about Teresa myself. This time I thought the girls in the canoe were Mom and Dulcie, but I wasn't sure. I still couldn't see anyone's face clearly.

Between the sighing of the wind and the dark day, I felt lonely and sad. In an effort to escape my mood, I opened *To Kill a Mockingbird*. I was more than halfway through, but I hadn't read much before I fell asleep with my head on the open book.

The sound of the back door opening woke me up. I turned and saw Sissy standing a couple of feet away. She was still wearing Emma's red sweatshirt.

"What are *you* doing here?" I didn't bother to hide my annoyance. "Emma's asleep, but even if she was wide awake, I wouldn't let you near her."

"I didn't come to see Emma. I came to see *you*."

"Why?"

She twirled the sweatshirt hood's drawstring. "I didn't have anything else to do."

"Well, *I* have plenty to do."

"Like what?"

"Like read this book, for one thing."

Sissy craned her neck to see the title. "*To Kill a Mockingbird*. I never read that. Is it good?"

Determined to ignore her, I held the book in front of my face and tried to read.

"I guess you're mad about what I said yesterday," she mumbled.

I lowered the book. "Why did you tell Emma those stories? She had bad dreams all night. That's why she's still asleep."

"She shouldn't be such a fraidy cat," Sissy said. "I was just kidding around."

"That's what you said when you almost drowned her."

Sissy shrugged. "I guess I'm the only one around here with a sense of humor."

"If you think that kind of stuff is funny, you're sick."

She laughed. "At least I don't read books about bird killers. *That's* pretty sick, if you ask me."

"You are so ignorant," I said in a nasty voice. "*To Kill a Mockingbird* isn't about bird killers."

Sissy sat down at the table across from me. "What *is* it about, then?"

"I haven't finished reading it yet, have I?" I marked my place and laid the book down. "It's required summer reading for eighth grade. I have to pass a test and write an essay on it when school starts."

"Big deal. I hate school. I'm glad I don't have to go anymore."

"What do you mean? You're too young to quit school."

"I mean for the summer, stupid. I'm on vacation. Like everybody—including you." Sissy tilted her chair back so far I was sure she'd fall on her head any second. Not that I cared. Maybe she'd leave if she hurt herself.

"How's Dulcie this morning?" she asked. "Are her paintings ruined?"

"Why should *you* care?"

Sissy rocked back and forth on the chair's legs, as if she were trying to figure out how far she could go without tipping over. "I wish I could've seen her face when she found that mess. I would've laughed and laughed."

"It *was* you!" Sure I was right, I glared at Sissy. "*You* wrecked the studio, didn't you? And then you made up all that stuff about Teresa!"

"You're crazy," Sissy said. "Why would I do something like that?"

"Because you're a spiteful little brat!"

At that point, Sissy finally overbalanced the chair and crashed to the floor. She made such a loud noise, I jumped up, scared my wish had come true and she'd really hurt herself. "Are you okay?"

She rubbed the back of her head and threw my own words back at me. "Why should *you* care?" Without waiting for an answer, she went to the back door. "I'm going for a walk. You can come if you like."

I stared at her in disbelief. "What makes you think I'd go anywhere with you?"

"I want to show you something." Sissy gave me one of her sly smiles. "I guarantee you won't be sorry."

When I hesitated, she added, "You're always asking me questions—where do I live, what's my last name, personal stuff like that. If you really want to know, come with me. Maybe I'll tell you."

Maybe you will, I thought. *Probably you won't.* Giving in to curiosity, I glanced at the kitchen clock. Nine o'clock. Emma would sleep for at least another hour. "I can't go far," I said. "Emma will be worried if she wakes up and nobody's home."

"Plus you don't want to get in trouble with your crazy aunt," Sissy added.

With a shrug, I let her lead me outside and into the pine woods. We walked single file along a narrow path that wound around trees, roots, and mossy boulders bearded with ferns. Mosquitoes hummed in my ears, and gnats circled my head. Except for the cries of gulls and crows, it was very quiet.

"Where are we going?" I asked.

"To a place I know."

We came out of the woods on a hill above the lake. Down below, the water lay still and calm, as gray as the sky above it.

Sissy walked to the end of a rocky overhang and dropped to her knees, right on the edge. "What I want to show you is down there." She pointed at the lake.

"You'd better come back. You might fall." I spoke loudly, so she wouldn't guess I was afraid of high places.

A gust of wind swirled through her hair and lifted the hood of her sweatshirt. "Fraidy cat." She leaned farther out, crouched like a gargoyle on the rock. "I'm the only one who knows what's down there."

"Oh, sure." Sick of her grin, sick of her show-off personality, sick of everything about her, even her bathing suit, I backed away from her and the scary place she'd led me.

"I thought you wanted me to tell you my secrets," she taunted in a singsong voice. "Sissy, Sissy, where do you live? What's your mommy like, what's your daddy like? What's your last name? Oh, Sissy, Sissy, tell me your secrets."

I put more distance between us. "I'm going home. Emma's probably awake now. She'll wonder where I am."

"You're as big a baby as she is." Sissy got to her feet and walked toward me. "Are you scared I'm going to push you off the cliff?" She lunged at me as if she really meant to do it. When I jumped backward, she laughed. "Baby, baby, baby."

"Go away!" I yelled at her. "I never want to see you again."

She met my eyes dead on, giving me the full benefit of the cold stare she was so good at. The wind toyed with her hair, whipping pale strands across her tan face. "You can't get rid of me . . . even if you try."

High above our heads, the tall pines swayed and murmured. A gull cried. Waves splashed against the lake's rocky shore. Drops of rain began to fall.

With a laugh, Sissy shoved me aside and darted off into the rain. "So long," she called. "Goodbye, ta-ta, adieu."

I watched her for a few moments, and then I followed her. If she wouldn't tell me where she lived, I'd find out myself. I'd go right up to her door and tell her mother that Sissy wasn't welcome at Gull Cottage anymore.

As little and skinny as she was, Sissy was fast. I couldn't keep her in sight, try as hard as I could. Just as I was about to give up, I glimpsed her, far ahead, disappearing into a grove of tall pines. By the time I reached the shelter of the trees, the rain was pouring down and Sissy had disappeared.

I looked around, bewildered. Where had she gone? There was nothing here. Just pines and tall grass and tangles of wild roses and vines growing over outcrops of mossy stones.

When I heard a car whoosh past, I ran through the pines to a road. On the other side, I saw a small yellow house with blue shutters and a curl of smoke coming from its chimney. A rock garden and beds of flowers bloomed around the porch, their colors brightening the gloom.

I ran across and knocked on the door, sure I'd found Sissy's home. She'd be surprised to see me on *her* doorstep for a change.

Inside, a dog began barking and someone said, "Hush, Chauncy." The door opened, and a woman peered at me. "Yes?"

The dog kept barking. He was large and brown and had a plumy tail, but he didn't look especially fierce. Just noisy.

"Is Sissy home?" I asked.

"Sissy?" The woman shook her head, puzzled. "I don't know anybody by that name." Turning back to the dog, she said, "Be quiet!"

Chauncy regarded her with mournful eyes and lay down, head on his paws, as if he were ashamed of himself. His tail thumped the floor.

"That's better," the woman told him, and his tail thumped harder. "Now," she said to me, "you'd better come in and dry off. You're soaked."

I hesitated a second, but I was cold, drenched, and worn out from chasing Sissy. The woman had a friendly look, and the dog was quite sweet now that he'd stopped barking. The room beyond the open door looked warm and cozy—and dry.

"My name's Kathie Trent," the woman said. "But I don't believe I know you."

"I'm Ali O'Dwyer. I'm staying with my aunt Dulcie at Gull Cottage."

She nodded. "Jeanine Donaldson told me Dulcie was back."

"Do you know my aunt?"

"I haven't seen her since she was about your age, maybe younger." She looked at me closely. "You're shivering. Let's get you dried off before you catch pneumonia."

I followed Ms. Trent to the bathroom. Handing me a towel, she said, "There's a robe on the back of the door. Put that on, and I'll toss your clothes in the dryer. Then you can tell me all about yourself—and Dulcie and Claire, too."

Soon I was bundled up in a fluffy bathrobe, sitting near a small wood stove and sipping hot tea. Chauncy dozed near my feet, and Ms. Trent sat across from me in a rocking chair. She wore her gray hair in a long braid down her back, but her face was unlined and rosy. Her jeans were faded, and her gray sweatshirt was several sizes too big; however, I could tell she was as slim as Dulcie, even though she was older.

She regarded me over the rim of her teacup. "No one here thought Dulcie or Claire would ever come back to the lake."

Here we go again, I thought. Aloud I said, "I guess Mrs. Donaldson told you she came to see Dulcie."

Ms. Trent nodded and waited for me to go on.

"Dulcie didn't remember her, but she was friendly at first. Then Mrs. Donaldson mentioned Teresa, and Dulcie got upset.

She said she didn't remember her, either, and went off in a huff." I tied the robe's belt tighter.

"It was really embarrassing," I went on, "but Mrs. Donaldson was very nice about it—she even apologized for upsetting Dulcie."

"Jeanine's a sweet person," Ms. Trent said.

Unlike Dulcie, I added silently. "Mrs. Donaldson knew Teresa. Did you know her, too?" I asked.

"Yes, I did." Ms. Trent took a sip of tea. "I hate to say it, but her older sister, Linda, and I spent a lot of time running away from the poor kid. Teresa wanted to tag along everywhere we went, but she was five or six years younger—a big difference when you're a teenager and your little sister is ten. If we left her out, she'd tattle on Linda just to get her in trouble."

She leaned back in the rocking chair and watched the rain run down the windowpanes. "It's an awful thing to say, but I don't think anyone liked Teresa—kids or adults. She was just too difficult. Always mad about something. From what Jeanine says, she caused so much trouble between Dulcie and Claire that your grandmother used to send her home."

She sighed. "After what happened, I've often wished I'd been nicer to her. She couldn't have been very happy."

For a while we sat quietly. I thought about Caroline Hogan—in third grade everybody hated her, I don't remember why now. Then she got hit by a car. She didn't die or anything, but when I saw her on crutches, I felt terrible. If something bad happened to Sissy, I guessed I'd feel the same way. Maybe I'd try to be nicer the next time I saw her. *Maybe.*

As I sipped my tea, I stared at the quilt hanging on the wall across from me. It was done in shades of blues and grays ranging from dark to light, and its patterns swirled like water. The quilt had a melancholy feeling, sad beyond words. It reminded me of Dulcie's lake paintings.

Ms. Trent turned to see what I was looking at. "That's my interpretation of the lake," she said, "its colors, its currents, its depth. One of my best pieces, I think, but no one has ever offered to buy it. Several people say it's too depressing. The blues and the grays . . ." With a shrug, she tilted back in the rocker and drank her tea.

"Is it true Teresa's body was never found?" I asked.

"Did Jeanine tell you that?"

"No, Sissy did—the girl I was looking for."

Ms. Trent sighed. "The lake often keeps its dead. The water's deep, you know, and dark. The bottom's rocky. Bodies get caught under ledges. . . ." Her voice trailed off. "Well, there's no sense dwelling on the morbid details. It was a sad end to an unhappy child's life."

I tucked the robe around my feet and curled up as small as I could. I wanted to let go of Teresa, but I had more questions.

"Sissy also told me Mom and Dulcie were in the canoe with Teresa the day she drowned. She said it was their fault—that they murdered Teresa."

Ms. Trent set her teacup down with a tiny clink. "There was a lot of talk at the time. Teresa's parents were sure Dulcie and Claire were involved. They even got the police to talk to your mother and aunt, but nothing came of it." She paused. "In case you're wondering, I think Teresa took the canoe out on a whim, and that Dulcie and Claire had nothing to do with it."

I reached down to pet Chauncy. Without raising my head, I asked, "Do people ever say they've seen Teresa's ghost?"

"Of course not." Ms. Trent laughed. "Did Sissy tell you that, too?"

"She scared my cousin, Emma, half to death." *And me, too.*

"I wonder who that child is," Ms. Trent mused. "Do you know her last name?"

"She won't tell me. I don't even know where she lives. That's why I followed her today." I frowned. "I want to find her house so Dulcie can talk to her mother. Sissy's a bad influence on Emma. She ought to stay away from us."

A clock struck eleven times like a miniature Big Ben, startling us both. I jumped up, stricken with guilt. I'd walked off two hours ago and left Emma sleeping. Dulcie was probably furious. "Are my clothes dry? I have to go home."

Ms. Trent disappeared into the laundry room and came back with my jeans and T-shirt and underwear, still warm from the dryer.

"It's raining too hard to walk all the way back to Gull Cottage," she said as she handed them to me. "Why don't you call Dulcie? I'd love to see her. I'd drive you myself, but my poor Volvo's in the shop having yet another overhaul."

As soon as I was dressed, I dialed Dulcie's number. Just as I'd feared, she was cross at me for leaving without a word to anyone. But she was also relieved I was safe.

"I'll come right away. Where are you?"

"At Ms. Trent's. It's a yellow house on Sycamore Road. She has flowers everywhere, more even than Mom has. You can't miss it."

"What on earth are you doing there?"

"I tried to follow Sissy home, but I couldn't keep up with her. I thought she must live in Ms. Trent's house, so I knocked on the door and she invited me in, but she doesn't know Sissy."

"Sissy, Sissy, Sissy." Dulcie sighed into the phone. "I wish you'd never met that girl."

After she hung up, I sat down on the sofa. My aunt wasn't the only one who wished I'd never met Sissy. Chauncy nudged my knee with his nose and looked at me hopefully. I petted him, and Ms. Trent laughed.

"He'll expect you to keep that up for hours," she said. "I've never had a dog who needed more love than Mr. Chauncy."

A few minutes later, Dulcie's car pulled into the driveway next to the cottage. I glimpsed Emma in the back seat, her face pressed against the window.

Despite all attempts to silence him, Chauncy ran to the door and barked loudly, just as he had when I'd arrived.

Ms. Trent greeted Dulcie. "Ignore that silly dog. He never bites."

Dulcie carried Emma inside. "Don't put me down," Emma begged. "I'm scared of dogs."

"His name's Chauncy," I told Emma. "He's an old sweetie pie. See?" I petted Chauncy and he leaned against my legs, huffing happily.

"I don't like dogs," Emma said.

In the meantime, Ms. Trent was introducing herself to Dulcie. "I'm Kathie Trent," she said, "but you'd have known me as Kathie Miller. My folks worked at Lake View Cabins, way back when the Abbotts owned the place."

Dulcie ran her fingers through her rain-dampened hair, but nothing she did could tame it. "I'm sorry but—"

"It's been a long time," Ms. Trent said.

"My memory's terrible." Dulcie looked around the cottage, her eyes caught by the quilts. "These are beautiful. Did you make them?"

"Yes, I did." Ms. Trent smiled. "Ali tells me you're a painter. I'd love to see your work someday."

Dulcie shifted Emma so she could reach into her purse for a business card. "I'm in the studio every day, a converted boathouse down on the shore. It's a lovely spot to work."

"That's the lake." Emma pointed at the blue and gray quilt. "All deep and dark and scary."

"What a perceptive child," Ms. Trent said, clearly impressed.

"What's perscective mean?" Emma asked.

"'Perceptive' means you understand stuff," I told her.

"I do understand stuff," Emma agreed. "Lots of stuff."

"We'd better go," Dulcie said. "Thanks for sheltering my errant niece. I hope she wasn't a nuisance."

"Ali's welcome anytime," Ms. Trent said, "as are you and the perceptive Emma."

As soon as we were in the car, Dulcie let me have it. "It was extremely irresponsible to go off and leave Emma alone. If you do anything like that again, I'll find someone else to take care of my daughter. Someone who's more mature than you are."

"I'm sorry," I mumbled. "But Sissy—"

"Stop blaming Sissy for everything," Dulcie cut in. "You're thirteen years old. Act like it."

Stung into silence, I slumped in the front seat and gazed out the rain-streaked window. Dulcie stared straight ahead, her face closed, her hands tight on the wheel.

Strapped in her child seat in the back, Emma was unusually quiet. The only sound was the *slappity-slap* of the windshield wipers and the hiss of rain under the tires.

~ 14 ~

Gradually, Dulcie got over being angry at me, probably because Sissy stayed away. I read to Emma, played games with her, and, when the sun finally came out, took her swimming. We painted pictures and made things with clay—lopsided pots, oddly shaped animals, dishes and cups that Dulcie fired in the kiln. I tried making my shell-and-stone displays, and Dulcie liked them. She said I was an artist, too—it obviously ran in the family.

After more than a week had passed without Sissy, I began hoping she was gone for good. Moved, found someone else to torment—I didn't care where she was or where she'd gone. Just so she didn't come back.

One afternoon, Emma and I were sitting at the picnic table, fooling around with clay. The sun was hot. Perspiration soaked the hair on the back of my neck. Bumblebees buzzed and hummed to themselves in the hollyhocks. A mosquito whined in my ear, and another bit my arm.

Just as I was about to suggest a swim, Emma turned to me, her face thoughtful. "I wonder what Sissy's doing now."

"After the way she acted last time, I don't care what she's doing. Not one bit. Not even a teeny tiny smidgen of a split atom."

I exaggerated to make Emma laugh, but she didn't even smile. Bending her head over her clay pot, she said, "Sissy promised she'd come see me today."

"How could she tell you that? We haven't seen her for over a week."

Ignoring me, Emma concentrated on rolling a coil of clay between her hands, making it long and smooth like a glistening snake.

I lifted her chin and forced her to look at me. "Has Sissy been here?"

Emma jerked away from me. Dropping the coil of clay, she flattened it with her fist. "Squish," she said. "Squash. No more snake."

With a Sissy smirk on her face, she ran into the house. The screen door slammed shut behind her. A squirrel, frightened by the sound, scurried up a tree trunk and disappeared into the leaves. From somewhere in his green hiding place, he chitter-chattered his outrage.

Emma hadn't answered my question, but she didn't have to. The way she acted told me she'd managed to see Sissy without my knowing. But how? I was with her all the time—except when she took her nap and went to bed at night. I doubted Sissy was allowed out after dark, so she must be sneaking into Emma's room in the afternoon.

If that's what was going on, I'd soon put a stop to it. The sneaky little brat wasn't welcome here—and she knew it. Leaving my clay cat baking in the sun, I went inside to talk to Emma.

She was lying on the couch, her face bored and sulky—in a Sissy mood, for sure. "Has Sissy been sneaking in here while you're supposed to be taking a nap?"

"That's for me to know and you to find out." Emma's voice sounded just like Sissy's, mocking and spiteful.

I grabbed her shoulders and gave her a little shake. "I don't want her in this house. And neither does your mother!"

Emma pulled away from me. "Sissy's right. You're jealous because I like her better than I like you."

Disgusted with Emma, I stalked off to the kitchen and poured myself a glass of iced tea. Just as I sat down to drink it, Dulcie came in. She didn't say hello. She didn't smile. In fact, she didn't even look at me. She went straight to the coffeemaker and started a pot brewing.

While she waited, she turned to me. "Where's Emma?"

Annoyed by her tone of voice, I kept my eyes on the *New Yorker* I'd been reading. "She's sulking in the living room."

Dulcie sighed in exasperation. "What's going on between you two? Why can't you get along with each other?"

Like bad weather, I sensed blame coming my way again. "It's not my fault—"

"Oh, no, it's never your fault. It's Sissy's fault or Emma's fault. Maybe it's the weather's fault—it's too hot, too cold, too rainy. But it's not *your* fault. You aren't to blame for anything."

Hurt by her sarcasm, I started to cry. At the same moment, Dulcie reached into the cupboard for a coffee mug and dropped it. It shattered on the kitchen floor.

The noise brought Emma running. "What was that?" she asked from the doorway.

Dulcie was down on her knees gathering up bits of china. "I broke a cup. That's all."

"Why's Ali crying?"

Dulcie looked at me, her face stricken. Getting to her feet, she gave me a quick hug. "I'm so sorry, sweetie. I shouldn't have snapped at you like that." She looked past me at the lake, darkening now under a parade of clouds drifting across the sky.

"Everything's wrong," she muttered as she dumped the remains of the cup in the garbage. "You and Emma quarrel constantly, I can't sleep, I . . ." Finishing the sentence with a shrug, she reached for another cup and filled it with coffee.

I felt like saying she probably drank too much coffee, but I bit my tongue. She was already on edge, jumpy and jittery. It wouldn't take much to make her angry again.

"Your mother was right," she went on. "Coming here was a mistake. My paintings are terrible, too bad to show. I do the same thing over and over again—the lake, the fog. . . . They're hideous, but I can't paint anything else, just the dark water, the dark sky, and the—"

She broke off, sat down at the kitchen table, and covered her face with her hands. Emma patted her mother's shoulder, stroked her hair, and whispered, "Mommy, Mommy, don't cry. Everything will be okay."

Emma sounded like herself again, sweet, comforting, all traces of Sissy gone.

Keeping her face in her hands, Dulcie muttered, "I'm beginning to think we should close up the cottage and go home. Maybe I'll paint better in New York, in my own studio, away from all this water and wind and rain."

Emma drew back. "We can't leave," she cried, her voice suddenly shrill in the quiet kitchen. "We can't, we can't, we can't. Sissy—"

Dulcie seized Emma's shoulders. "Do you know how sick I am of hearing that child's name? Ever since you met her, there's been nothing but trouble between you and Ali. I don't want her coming here. I don't want you playing with her. Do you understand?"

Emma shrank away from Dulcie's angry face. I thought she'd cry, but her lip jutted out and she looked at her mother, defying her. "Sissy's my friend! I won't stop playing with her! You can't make me!"

Dulcie leapt to her feet and drew back her hand. I cringed, sure that she was going to slap Emma. Emma must have thought the same thing because she raised her arm to protect her face. "Don't hit me," she cried. "Don't hit me!"

Dulcie threw herself back down in the chair and began to sob. Emma looked at me, clearly frightened by her mother's behavior. Scared myself, I took Emma's hand. I was used to my mother behaving like this, but not Dulcie.

In a moment or two, Dulcie managed to control herself. Wiping her tears away with the back of her hand, she pulled Emma into her lap. "I'm sorry," she whispered. "Sometimes I don't know what gets into me."

With a sigh, she pushed her hair back from her face. "Why don't we get dinner started? Spaghetti, maybe. How would you two like that?"

In a voice so low that Dulcie didn't hear, Emma muttered, "I'm sick of spaghetti, and I'm sick of Ali, and I'm sick of Mommy."

I looked at her, but she turned away, hiding her face.

Making cheerful noises with pots and pans, Dulcie and I began fixing the meal. I boiled water and dropped in spaghetti. Dulcie whipped up tomato sauce, and Emma got out the bread and butter. My job was tossing spaghetti noodles at the wall. If they stuck, they were ready. Mom would never have let me do something like that.

At dinner, we sat together at the table, laughing and talking as if the earlier scenes had never happened. Emma ate most of her spaghetti. No one mentioned Sissy. Instead, we planned a hike and picnic in the state park, as well as another trip to Pemaquid Point.

But when darkness came, and I lay in bed alone, I found myself thinking about Dulcie. Before we came to Gull Cottage,

I'd never seen her angry or upset, never imagined her crying over anything. She was my tough New York City aunt, my artist aunt, my sophisticated, worldly aunt, smart and talented, witty and quick and daring—everything I wanted to be someday.

But now . . . well, I didn't know what to think. The longer we stayed here, the more she reminded me of Mom.

Gradually, I drifted into the Teresa dream: rough dark water, gray sky, fog. Three girls huddled in a canoe, quarreling, rocking the canoe. The fog thickened, hiding everything. A splash. A cry—I woke, terrified, clutching the old teddy bear.

Rain blew in the open window by my bed and struck my face. Shivering with cold, I leapt up and closed the window. In the sudden silence, I heard Emma shouting as if she, too, had awakened suddenly from a bad dream.

Wrapping a quilt around my shoulders, I ran to the top of the steps.

Emma stood in the hall below me. "Where's Mommy?"

"Isn't she in her room?"

"No." Emma began to cry. "I had a bad dream and I went to get her and she wasn't there."

I hurried down the stairs and checked Dulcie's room. Emma followed me, clinging to one hand. The empty bed was a mess of kicked-back sheets and blankets, and the window was wide open. I slammed it shut and went to the front door.

"She must be in the studio," I told Emma. "You stay here, and I'll go look."

I tried to pull my hand free, but Emma held tight. "Take me with you."

"But it's dark and rainy. The steps are slippery. You might fall."

"Don't leave me here," she begged. "The bones will get me."

I tried to calm her down, but she was crying too loudly to listen.

"Okay, okay," I said. "You can come, but be careful on the steps."

Still sobbing, Emma let me help her into her slicker. After I pulled mine on, I grabbed a flashlight and led her out into the rain and dark. Above the wind, I heard waves smashing against the shore. Thunder cracked and lightning flashed.

Emma pressed her face into my side. "I hate thunder," she whimpered.

By now, we were at the top of the stairs. Slowly and cautiously, we inched downward, feeling our way from step to step like blind people.

Lights shone from the boathouse windows. Without knocking, I opened the door, and Emma and I stumbled over the threshold.

Dulcie spun around and stared at us, her eyes momentarily wide with fright. "What are you doing here?" she cried. "You scared me bursting in like that!"

"I had a bad dream." Emma began crying harder. "I couldn't find you, you weren't in your bed—you weren't anywhere."

While Dulcie comforted Emma, I studied her paintings. What she'd said about them was true. They leaned against the walls, tall, narrow canvases, maybe three feet by seven feet, stark and ugly. She'd covered all of them with streaks of blue and gray washed on in thin layers. Then she'd added clumsy daubs of black and splashes of reds and dark blues and purples.

What really scared me, though, was the pale blob at the bottom of each painting. A stone, a shell, a skull—too blurry to be sure what it was.

I certainly wouldn't have wanted one of those paintings in my house. Not if I wanted to feel good or sleep well. They looked as if they'd been vandalized again—only this time Dulcie had done the damage herself.

My aunt caught me looking at the paintings. "I couldn't sleep," she said in a flat voice. "The storm kept me awake. I thought I might get some work done, but . . ." She shrugged. "Just being here depresses me."

"They scare me." Emma hid her face against her mother's side. "Don't let me see them."

Dulcie freed herself from Emma and turned the paintings so they faced the wall. "Let's go to bed," she said in a low, toneless voice.

Silently, Emma and I followed Dulcie out into the storm. As we climbed the stairs to the cottage, I glanced over my shoulder. For a second, I thought I saw someone on the dock watching us. I blinked the rain from my eyes and looked again. No one was there. Waves pounded the shore, and the wind blew in gusts.

"Come on, Ali," Dulcie called from above. "You'll catch your death in this rain."

Catch your death. I'd never thought about it before, but suddenly the expression made no sense. *Catch your death, Catch your death,* I repeated, as I climbed the steps to the cottage. Wasn't it the other way around? Didn't death catch you?

Shivering with cold and fear, I was tempted to ask Dulcie if I could sleep with her instead of going upstairs to my lonely room. But I was thirteen—surely too old to be scared of the dark. So I went to bed alone and read *To Kill a Mockingbird* until the sky began to lighten behind the clouds.

─◌15◌─

The next day, the sun shone, but Dulcie's mood didn't lighten. She frittered the morning away drinking coffee and puttering around the cottage. In the afternoon, she took a long walk alone, despite Emma's plea to go with her.

"Sorry," she said. "I need time to myself."

Emma and I watched her stride away up the cliff path. When she was out of sight, Emma said, "I hope Sissy comes over today."

"You heard your mother. She doesn't want you to play with Sissy." I sighed. "Besides, we have more fun together when she's not here."

Emma pulled a rose off a bush by the door and twirled it in her fingers, wincing when a thorn pricked her. "You don't know *anything* about Sissy."

She pulled the rose apart and scattered its pink petals on the grass, where they lay like confetti. Then without another word, she ran inside, letting the screen door slam in my face. I yanked it open, and she retreated to the doorway of her room. "You better not hit me," she shouted. "I'll tell Mommy!"

"Why would I hit you?" I stared at her, perplexed.

"Because you're hateful!"

"Emma—" I began, but she closed her door.

"Don't come in here!" she cried from inside. "Go away!"

I retreated to the kitchen, a total failure as a babysitter. I couldn't do anything right. Not for Emma. And not for Dulcie, either. My aunt was in a perpetual bad mood. Irritable, jumpy, tense—all because her paintings weren't going well. As if that was *my* fault.

While I stood at the window, brooding on my miserable vacation, it started raining. Another cold, gray day in Maine. Summer-school algebra would have been more fun than Sycamore Lake.

I looked at the phone hanging on the kitchen wall. Maybe I should call Mom. She'd said I could come home if I was unhappy. I lifted the receiver and pushed 1 for long distance. Just as I was about to dial the area code, I caught sight of Emma crossing the lawn. What was she doing outside in the rain? I hung up quickly and ran to the back door just as she disappeared into the trees.

Instead of calling her to come back, I grabbed my slicker and followed her, sure she planned to meet Sissy. Ducking behind trees, I kept her bright pink jacket in sight.

She stopped in a gloomy grove of pine trees not far from me. Sissy was perched on a boulder, waiting for her. In the dim light, I could see that Sissy was holding something.

"You brought her!" Emma held out her hands, but Sissy thrust whatever she carried behind her back.

"You said I could play with her today," Emma protested.

"I didn't promise," Sissy said. "I said maybe you could. Just *maybe.*"

"Please, Sissy." Emma sounded close to tears.

Sissy wrinkled her forehead as if she were thinking hard. "If I let you play with her, will you promise to do everything I say?"

"Yes," Emma said.

"Cross your heart and hope to die?" Sissy asked.

Solemnly, Emma crossed her heart with one finger.

Sissy smiled and brought a doll from behind her back. Its hair was a dull greenish gray, brittle and caked with mud. Its face was discolored, and its ragged clothes were stained. I'd never seen a more hideous thing, but I recognized it.

And so did Emma. "Edith," she crooned, "Edith." She cradled the Lonely Doll in her arms. "Can I really keep her?"

"Just for a little while." Sissy came close and whispered in Emma's ear. Emma nodded, nodded again, and kept on nodding, agreeing to everything Sissy said.

Unable to stand it anymore, I jumped out from my hiding place and startled them both. "Give that ugly doll back to her, and don't do anything she tells you to!" I yelled at Emma.

"Who's your boss, Em?" Sissy asked. "Her or me?"

"You," Emma said. "You're the boss. I do what *you* say, Sissy, not what Ali says. Not what Mommy says."

I reached for the doll, intending to throw it at Sissy, but Emma was too fast for me. Holding it tightly, she ran to Sissy's side. "Go away, Ali. Sissy and me don't want to play with you."

"I don't want to play with *you*," I yelled as if I were eight instead of thirteen.

"Ali, are you shouting at Emma?"

I whirled around and saw Dulcie standing a few yards away on the cliff top. Sissy disappeared so fast you'd think the woods had gobbled her up. Emma ran to her mother.

"Ali was mean to me," Emma wailed. "Don't let her stay here. Send her home."

"What now?" Anger edged Dulcie's voice. "Here I am, just getting my head together, and here you are, out in the rain, soaking wet, and quarreling again. Can't you two ever get along? What's wrong with you, anyway?" The rain had curled her hair so tightly, it bushed around her face, making her look like a madwoman—scary, raging with anger, her wet clothes sticking to her skinny body.

Emma held up the doll. "Ali's jealous because Sissy gave me Edith."

Dulcie stared at the doll as if it had come from some dark, secret place. "Where did you get that?" she whispered. "God in heaven, Emma, tell me!"

Emma drew back from her mother, even more scared by her tone of voice than I was. "She belongs to Sissy. She said—"

Dulcie grabbed the doll's arm and pulled so hard she yanked it off. Losing her balance, she staggered backward. For a moment, I froze, sure she was going to fall off the cliff. Instead, she spun around and hurled the doll's arm into the water far below. With her back to us, she stared down at the lake.

"You broke Sissy's doll," Emma screamed. "She'll be mad!"

Dulcie turned to face Emma. "I told you not to play with that girl!"

"And I told you Sissy's my friend and I'll play with her if I want to!" Emma's face flushed with anger.

"You'll do what I tell you!" With one quick move, Dulcie grabbed Edith. Pivoting, she threw the doll off the cliff. "Filthy, horrible thing!"

"I hate you!" Emma screamed.

"That's enough!" Dulcie picked up Emma and headed for the cottage. I ran along behind them, barely able to keep up with Dulcie's long-legged stride.

Ahead of me, Emma yelled and protested and struggled to escape. Dulcie said nothing. Nor did she look back to see where I was.

Letting them get even farther ahead, I stopped and tried to pull myself together. I was shaking, not just from the rain and the wind but from the scene I'd just witnessed. Why had the doll upset Dulcie so much? She'd acted like a crazy woman, throwing the doll off the cliff as though it were a threat, something evil, dangerous. The scene replayed itself in my mind, over and over—Dulcie grabbing the doll from Emma, screaming, her hair flying around her face, hurling it into space. Strange as it seemed, my aunt had clearly been terrified of that filthy, water-stained doll.

At that moment, standing alone in the rain and the wind, I wanted my mother more than I'd ever wanted anyone in my life. I also wanted my father, my house, my room, my friends. Emma's behavior scared me—and so did Dulcie's.

Soaked and shivering, I ran to the cottage. Emma's bedroom door was closed, but I could hear Dulcie saying, "That doll wasn't fit to touch, let alone play with."

"It was Sissy's," Emma wailed. "You threw Sissy's doll away!"

With a sigh, I trudged up to my room. Rain drummed on the roof, and thunder still rumbled in the distance. I thought again about calling Mom and asking to come home. All that stopped me was the thought that she'd say, *I told you you'd hate the lake.*

I stayed in my room for at least an hour, hoping Dulcie might come up to see if I was all right. Downstairs, all was silent. Not a sob, not a voice. The only sound was the mournful murmur of the wind in the pines outside.

I tried to read, but my room was cold. Shadows gathered in the corners. I began thinking someone was hiding in the dark place by the closet, breathing slowly in and out, in and out. Every time I looked, I was sure I'd just missed seeing who it was.

Unable to stand it anymore, I ran downstairs. Dulcie huddled under a blanket on the couch, reading an art magazine. When she saw me, she put her finger to her mouth and beckoned me to follow her to the kitchen.

The moment the door closed behind me, Dulcie said, "Why did you let Emma go out in the rain? Don't you have any sense?"

"I didn't *let* her go anywhere," I said. "She went to her room, and the next thing I knew she was running across the field toward the woods. She must have climbed out her window or something. Sissy was waiting—"

"Leave Sissy out of this," Dulcie broke in. "Emma is *your* responsibility, Ali."

Without answering, I turned my back to hide the tears in my eyes. It wasn't fair to blame me. I was trying hard to take care of my cousin—no easy task with Sissy around. Why couldn't Dulcie see that?

For a few minutes, the only sound was the endless rain and the ticking clock. The kitchen was shadowy, the yellow paint dull and cheerless. At that moment, I hated Gull Cottage and the lake and the bad weather. It was all I could do not to call my mother to come and get me.

Suddenly, my aunt broke the silence. "I'm sorry, Ali. I don't know what's wrong with me. I'm just not myself. I can't do anything right anymore. I can't sleep, can't paint, can't be a good mother—or a good aunt, either."

She sounded close to tears herself, and when I looked at her, I saw my mother in my aunt's face. "It's okay," I mumbled, even though it wasn't. Saying something mean and then claiming you're not yourself doesn't take the hurt away.

"I don't understand why that doll upset me so much," Dulcie said slowly. "I used to buy ugly, dirty old dolls at flea markets and make them into sculptures. Remember? I had dozens of them. Fifty or more."

I'd forgotten those dolls until now. Dulcie had taken them apart and put them back together, creating monsters like

Frankenstein—a leg from one, a head from another, mismatched arms. Some were bald, others eyeless. She often replaced their bodies with boxes filled with strange objects—hard little tinfoil hearts, pebbles, shells, beads, tiny scissors from charm bracelets, sheets of paper with cryptic words written on them, bits of broken china, pennies, knives, nails. Many of them had holes in their heads with springs, feathers, twigs, or dead flowers poking out of them. The scariest had no heads at all. As a finishing touch, she often spray-painted them with a thin coat of green paint, giving them the appearance of things exhumed from graves or the depths of the sea.

"I didn't like them," I admitted. "They scared me."

"They weren't pretty," Dulcie said with a small smile. "But, believe it or not, they sold pretty well."

The smile faded. Dulcie twisted a strand of hair around her finger and pulled it tight. "After Emma was born, I stopped making them," she said. "I painted and drew more, sculpted less. I thought I'd outgrown my dark stage. But now . . ." She shrugged her thin shoulders. "You've seen what I'm doing. Dark. Very dark."

"The people who bought your dolls might like those paintings," I said a little doubtfully.

"Maybe." Dulcie sounded unconvinced. With a sigh, she got up and went to the door. "I'd better check on Emma. Why don't you open a can of soup for supper? Chicken with rice, maybe. We could use something warm and comforting."

She got to her feet, and I watched her walk away. The spring in her step was gone, and her shoulders drooped. She looked more like Mom than ever.

While I fixed the soup, I watched the rain fall, veiling the lake, blurring the line between water and sky. Images ran through my head—the cottage, the lake, the canoe, Teresa, the doll, my dream. And Sissy—frowning, angry, full of hatred. They were all connected, I was sure of it.

16

The next morning, Emma woke up complaining of a headache. Her face was flushed, and she was coughing. Dulcie touched Emma's forehead and hurried to the bathroom for the thermometer.

Emma's temperature was high enough for Dulcie to call a doctor. "She'll see us at eleven," Dulcie told me. "Do you want to come along?"

I peered out at the rain, still pouring down. The cottage was cozy and dry, and I had no desire to go anywhere. I held up *To Kill a Mockingbird*. "I absolutely have to finish this before school starts."

After Dulcie and Emma left, I made myself comfortable on the sofa and opened my book. I was relieved to see I'd finished at least two thirds of it.

I hadn't read more than a dozen pages when I heard a knock at the door. I looked up and saw it was Sissy. Before I had a chance to tell her to go away, she walked into the house as if she owned it.

I closed my book with an angry snap. "Who invited you in?"

"Me, myself, and I."

"Well, me, myself, and I *disinvite* you." I hoped to sound even more sarcastic than she did.

Perching on the old wicker armchair across from me, Sissy

made it clear she wasn't leaving. "Look what I found floating in the lake." She pulled Edith from under her wet sweatshirt and thrust her at me.

I drew back with distaste. "Get that thing away from me."

Sissy's lips curled up in a foxy grin. "I saw Dulcie yank Edith's arm off and throw her off the cliff. Why do you think she got so riled up?"

"Dulcie didn't want Emma playing with a dirty, disgusting doll." I kept my face as blank as I could so Sissy wouldn't know I'd wondered the same thing.

"You know what? Edith looked like a dead body floating in the water." Sissy waved the doll in my face. "And you know what else? I bet Teresa looked just like Edith after Dulcie pushed her into the lake."

I tightened my grip on my book to keep myself from throwing it at her. "Get out of here!"

Sissy leaned over me, close enough for her damp, stringy hair to brush my cheek, close enough for me to smell its stale, doggy odor. "I know you hate me, but I'm not going anywhere till I feel like it."

"You ought to wash your hair," I said. "It stinks."

"You don't smell so good yourself." Clutching Edith, Sissy made a face and dashed out the door into the rain. "Catch me if you can, Ali Ali Alligator!"

As before, she ran into the woods and took the trail along the cliff top. Once again, I followed her. I had to find out where she lived and who she was. If her mother knew how much trouble her daughter caused, she'd keep her at home, make her stay away from Gull Cottage. With no Sissy to spoil things, Emma, Dulcie, and I might actually have fun again.

At first, I had no trouble keeping Sissy in sight. The red sweatshirt flashed around bends in the trail and in and out of rocks and boulders. I ran behind her, keeping a decent distance between us. Just as I was beginning to think I'd be successful, she turned away from the lake and disappeared into that dark grove of pines where I'd lost her before.

Determined to find her, I walked slowly, listening for footsteps and looking for the red sweatshirt. Maybe it was the gloom of the day or the slow, sad murmur of the wind in the trees, but the grove seemed to grow darker and colder. Overhead, a crow cawed, and farther away another answered. I stopped, suddenly afraid.

That's when I realized where I was. The mossy rocks I'd noticed before were tombstones. Most were so old they blended into the trees and bushes, their inscriptions worn and covered with lichen. Some were newer, their names and dates still legible.

Scared almost witless, I ran toward the road. In my panic, I tripped on small headstones and tumbled to the ground more than once. Brambles caught my hair and scratched my arms, and pine branches whipped my face, but nothing slowed me down. I ran with all my strength.

Then I glimpsed what I'd been looking for—the red sweatshirt.

With a shout, I burst out of a grove of trees. "I see you, Sissy!"

But Sissy wasn't there. Like an offering, the red sweatshirt dangled from the hand of a stone angel.

Heart pounding, I looked around, sure she was hiding nearby, laughing at me. "Sissy?" I called, my voice unnaturally loud in the silent cemetery.

No one answered.

"Where are you?" I called again.

Still no answer. Not even a giggle.

"Stupid brat!" I yelled. "You can't scare me with your dumb tricks."

This time, crows answered, shattering the quiet with raucous cries.

Angry now, I walked right up to the angel. Sissy wasn't going to frighten me. Or make me look like an idiot. I'd show her.

But as I grabbed the sweatshirt, I noticed the words carved at the angel's feet.

In Memory of Our Beloved Daughter and Sister
Teresa Abbott
March 11, 1967 to July 19, 1977

May her soul rise from the deep and be at peace

Teresa, Teresa. The name ran round and round in my head like the words of a song you don't want to hear. *Teresa, Teresa,* the wind whispered while the raindrops beat out the rhythm.

The angel's blank eyes gazed at me, its hand reaching out as if to seize mine. I edged away, but the angel continued to stare at me, its marble face expressionless, stained from years of rain and snow.

Unable to bear those eyes, I ran toward the road, dodging headstones and trees. Somewhere behind me, I thought I heard Sissy laugh, but I didn't dare look back.

It wasn't until Ms. Trent opened her door that I realized I was still clutching the sweatshirt. I threw it down and flung myself, sobbing, into the woman's arms.

"Ali!" she said. "What's wrong?"

"I was in the graveyard up the road," I stammered. "I saw an angel there, a memorial for Teresa Abbott."

Ms. Trent nodded, but she was clearly puzzled. "The family erected it years ago."

"That sweatshirt was hanging from the angel's hand." I pointed at the wet, dirty heap on the floor. "Sissy left it there."

Ms. Trent stooped to pick up the sweatshirt. "I'm not sure what this is all about," she said, "but you're soaked, Ali—as usual." She laughed and shook her head. "You know the drill. Put on the robe and give me your wet clothes. I'll stick them in the dryer, along with the sweatshirt. When you're warm and dry, we'll talk."

A few minutes later, I was once again wrapped snugly in Ms. Trent's fluffy bathrobe. Chauncy sprawled on the floor near me, sighing contentedly from time to time. The warmth inside the cottage had steamed up the windows, but deep inside I was cold and shivery.

Ms. Trent handed me a cup of tea and sat down in her rocker. "Promise to visit me on a nice sunny day next time," she said with a smile.

A log in the stove shifted and fell. I watched Ms. Trent prod it into place with a poker. Firelight danced across her face, showing a fine network of wrinkles.

"What's wrong, Ali?" She looked at me kindly.

"What did Teresa look like?" I asked in such a low voice that Ms. Trent asked me to repeat the question. "Teresa Abbott— what did she look like?"

She thought a moment, as if trying to remember. "An ordinary kid, kind of plain," she said at last. "Skinny, small for her age. Sharp featured. Didn't smile often."

"Did she have blond hair?"

"Yes. Yes, she did. In the summer, it turned almost white." She smiled. "That was the only thing about Teresa I envied—her hair. When I was a teenager, I wanted to be a blond."

I huddled deeper into the soft sofa. "Was Teresa's sister, Linda, ever Miss Webster's Cove?"

"Yes, but—"

I interrupted. "Did she wear a tiara and ride in a motorboat parade and throw roses in the lake?"

"Did Dulcie tell you that?" Ms. Trent asked. "I didn't think she remembered anything."

"No, not her. Somebody else." I fidgeted with the bathrobe's sash, twirling it this way and that. What I was thinking couldn't be true—at least I hoped not. "Was Linda beautiful, and did she have lots of boyfriends?"

"Linda Abbott was the prettiest girl in high school. All the boys were in love with her." Ms. Trent took a sip of tea. "Has Jeanine been telling you about Linda?"

I shook my head. There was one more question. And it was the scariest one of all. Hoping she'd say no, I asked, "Did Linda ever call Teresa . . . 'Sissy'?"

Ms. Trent put her teacup down slowly. "Yes," she said slowly, as if remembering something long forgotten. "That was Linda's nickname for Teresa when she was little—Sissy."

I pulled the bathrobe tighter, but I couldn't stop shivering. Cold seeped in through every seam. My feet were frozen, and so were my hands. "Do you believe in ghosts?"

Ms. Trent looked at me, hands clasped, face serious, and slowly shook her head. "I know what you're thinking, Ali, but Sissy's a common nickname. That girl might be a troublemaker, but she's *not* Teresa."

"She looks like Teresa," I replied. "She acts like Teresa. She won't tell me her last name or where she lives. If I try to follow her, she disappears."

When I began to cry, Ms. Trent moved to the couch and put her arm around me. "I know you're upset, but you're letting your imagination run away with you. Sissy is Sissy—a real girl. She's not Teresa's ghost. It's impossible."

I wanted to snuggle into her side like a little kid, I wanted to believe her, I wanted to be comforted by her soft, reasonable voice. But no matter what excuses Ms. Trent made up, I knew what I knew.

"What about the sweatshirt?" I asked. "Sissy put it in the angel's hand because she wants me to know who she is."

"She left the sweatshirt there to scare you," Ms. Trent said, still calm, still reasonable. "You know—for a prank, a joke. It's exactly the sort of thing a girl like Sissy would do."

"That's what I thought at first, but . . ." I drew away from her side. "What if Mom and Dulcie were in the canoe with Sissy? What if they did something to her? What if she wants revenge?" My fears tumbled into words as I spoke.

Ms. Trent peered into my eyes. "What happened to Teresa was very sad. But this is the real world, Ali. You exist, I exist, millions of people exist. Ghosts do not exist—there's no room for them."

"You're wrong," I said, weeping. "You're wrong."

Ms. Trent tried to hug me again, but I shrugged her arm away. If she really wanted to comfort me, she'd believe me, she'd help me, she'd tell me what to do.

With a sigh, she got to her feet. "Your clothes must be dry. Why don't you get dressed, and I'll drive you home. My old Volvo seems to be working. At least for now."

Silently, I took my jeans and T-shirt, still warm from the dryer, and headed for the bathroom to change. Just as I closed the door, I heard the phone ring. Ms. Trent picked it up.

"Yes, Ali's here. I just told her I'd—"

Dulcie. What did she want? I yanked on my clothes and ran to Ms. Trent's side.

Ms. Trent handed me to the phone. "It's your aunt."

"Where is Emma?" Dulcie shouted into my ear.

"Isn't she with you?" I gripped the receiver, frightened by the panic in her voice.

"No! We came home, you weren't here, I gave Emma an antibiotic and put her to bed." Dulcie's words fell over each other and tangled themselves into a knot. "I just went to check on her. The window's open, and she's gone. Where would she go all by herself? It's raining, she has a fever, she should be in bed."

"I don't know where she is. I've been here —"

"If you'd been home, where you belong, she wouldn't be gone," Dulcie broke in. "Don't you ever think of anyone but yourself?"

"But, Dulcie, I—"

She slammed the receiver down with a bang that hurt my ear. "She's with Sissy!" I yelled into the phone, but of course she couldn't hear me.

Ms. Trent caught my arm as I ran toward the door. "Where are you going?"

"To find Emma!" I pulled free and dashed out into the rain.

"But the sweatshirt," she called after me. "Don't you want it?" Without answering, I darted across the road. If Emma was really with Sissy—and I was sure she was—she was in danger, and I had to save her.

17

Heart pounding, I raced back through the cemetery. Even though I didn't look at the angel, I sensed its blank eyes following me, its hand pointing the way to the lake and the cliff top.

Once I reached the path, I slowed down. The rain had changed to a heavy mist, and I could see only about three feet ahead. I didn't want to miss my way and fall off the rocks.

"Emma," I called. "Emma!"

There was no answer. Drops of water fell from the pines, gradually soaking my clothes. Now and then, I heard a gull cry, its voice sad and lonely. I was alone in a gray nothingness, no colors, no shapes.

At last, I heard Emma's high, piping voice. "Let's go back. I'm cold."

"Scaredy cat," Sissy taunted. "*Edith's* not afraid of the canoe. Why are you?"

I slid down a narrow path to the lake, scattering pebbles. The two of them looked up. Emma was surprised to see me, but Sissy grinned as if she'd been expecting me. Even if I'd wanted to, I couldn't have returned her smile. Now that I knew what she was, I didn't even want to look at her. She seemed as real and solid as ever, but I was scared she'd shed her skin the way I shed my clothes and stand before us in her true form—bones, nothing but bones, topped with a grinning skull and a tuft of hair, dressed in the rags of her bathing suit.

"Did you find the sweatshirt?" Sissy asked, mocking me with a sly grin. "I didn't want it anymore."

She stood knee-deep in the lake. Her faded bathing suit almost matched the fog, giving her an appropriately ghostly look. Beside her, an old canoe rode low in the water. Edith lay on the middle seat, her dirty face turned up to the foggy sky.

"Where did you get the canoe?" I asked.

Sissy shrugged, and the bones beneath her skin shifted. "It's just an old wreck of a thing. No one wants it. Not anymore."

Turning to Emma, she said, "Come on. Get in."

I grabbed my cousin's shoulder. "She's not going anywhere with you!"

Sissy laughed. "Want to bet?" Turning back to Emma, she held out the doll. "If you come with me, you can hold Edith."

Emma pulled free of my hands. Before I could stop her, she clambered into the canoe and sat on the middle seat, cradling Edith. "See? I'm not a scaredy cat baby like Ali."

Sissy jumped in and picked up the paddle. "There's room for you, too, Ali."

I splashed into the cold water and grabbed the side of the canoe. "Get out, Emma, and come home. You're sick, you've got a fever. Your mother doesn't know where you are. She's worried to death."

"Worried to death?" Sissy laughed. "What does Dulcie—or you—know about death?" Her eyes dared me to ask what *she* knew about death.

For Emma's sake, I kept my mouth shut. It would be better if my cousin never learned what her so-called friend really was. "Please." I grabbed her arm and tugged. The canoe rocked back and forth, and Emma clung to the sides.

"Stop, Ali," she cried. "You'll turn it over!"

Sissy dipped the paddle in the water. "Come or don't come," she said to me, "but I'm taking Emma for a ride."

Full of dread, I climbed into the canoe and took a seat in the front. With Emma sitting between us, Sissy paddled away from shore. In a moment, the mist surrounded us. Rocks and trees vanished as if they no longer existed. I could barely see Sissy and Emma, and I heard nothing but the gurgle and splash of the paddle moving through the water. It was like the dream I'd had of the three girls—only now it was real, and I was one of them.

Emma looked around uneasily. "Where are we going?" she said. "I can't see anything."

Sissy kept paddling.

"Take me home," Emma begged. "I don't like the canoe anymore. I don't like the fog. I want Mommy."

"Sorry, Em, but I don't know which way home is. Do you?" Sissy didn't pretend to be sorry or even worried. If anything, she seemed pleased with herself.

Emma began to cry. "Don't take me where the bones are. I don't want to see them."

"Bones, bones, bones," Sissy chanted. "Teresa wants you and Ali to visit her, stay with her awhile, keep her company."

"No," Emma cried.

I reached toward my cousin, but my arm wasn't quite long enough to touch her. I didn't dare move closer, for fear of upsetting the canoe.

"It's okay, Emma," I said. "She's just teasing you. We're almost home already." I hoped I was right, but I couldn't see the shore, a tree, the dock, or anything else.

Emma hugged the doll. "Me and Edith are scared."

Sissy laughed. "Give me Edith. She won't be scared if *I* hold her."

Emma clutched the horrid thing to her chest. "If I give her to you, will you take us home?"

"Maybe."

Emma turned to me. "Should I?"

"You'd better." Sissy answered before I had a chance to say a word.

Emma thrust the doll at Sissy. "Now take me home," she begged. "I'll do anything you say, just take me home."

Sissy sat still, the paddle in her hands, the doll beside her. "How bad do you want Edith?"

"Stop teasing her," I said. "Just take us home."

Sissy ignored me. "What if I throw Edith in the lake? Do you want her enough to jump in and get her?" She dangled the doll over the water. "Should I drop her?"

"No!" Emma cried. "No, Sissy, don't. Give her to me!"

I lunged past Emma at Sissy just as the doll flew out of her hands and splashed into the lake.

"Look what you made me do," Sissy yelled.

"I didn't make you do anything. You threw that doll—I saw you!"

While the two of us shouted at each other, Emma leaned out of the canoe, desperately reaching for the doll. Before I could stop her, she toppled into the lake. I saw her hair spread like seaweed on the surface—and then vanish. At the same moment, the canoe rocked wildly back and forth and tipped over.

As I plunged down into the cold dark water, I searched frantically for Emma. Through the murk, I glimpsed a swirl of hair, a pale face, an outstretched hand. Kicking hard, I swam toward her and grabbed her arm. The two of us sank together, weighed down by our wet clothes. Emma struggled like a fish trying to escape a net, but I held her tight.

I won't let you drown, I promised, *I'll save you. I'll save both of us.*

Using every bit of strength, I swam up toward the dim light of the gray sky. We came to the surface gasping for air. Emma clung to me, coughing and choking, too weak to struggle.

I swam to the overturned canoe and tried to get a good grip on it.

"Hold on," I told Emma.

"I can't," she wept. "I can't. It's too slippery."

"You have to!"

Just on the edge of the fog, Sissy circled us, drifting in and out of sight like a shark coming in for the kill. Slowly, she swam nearer, shoving the doll ahead of her.

I put my arms on either side of Emma to keep myself between her and Sissy. "Stay away from us!" I yelled.

Sissy pushed the doll closer. "It's nice in the water, Em. If you come swimming with me, I'll give you Edith—all yours forever. No takebacks."

Emma looked at me, and I shook my head. "You can't swim."

"Don't worry. I'll hold you up." Sissy swam close enough to grab Emma's hand. The doll floated nearby, her stained face barely visible in the dark water. "If you want to be my friend," she said, "you have to do what *I* say. Not what Ali says. Not what Dulcie says."

"Go away." Emma tugged her hand free of Sissy's grip. "I'm scared of you."

Shivering with cold and fear, I watched Sissy. Framed by long wet hair, her face was sharp and bony, her skin white, her eyes shadowy. The hands holding the doll were bony. If only she'd vanish into the water and sink to the bottom, where she belonged. If only Emma and I were safe in the cottage, drawing

132

or reading by the fire, warming ourselves with hot chocolate. If only, if only, if only. . . .

"Why are you here?" I whispered. "What do you want from us?"

Sissy swam even closer. Once more, I moved between her and Emma. I could hear my cousin's intake of breath. Her skin was cold.

"I want you to make Dulcie and Claire tell the truth," Sissy said. "They should be punished for what they did. It's not fair. They're grown up, and I'm—" She broke off and glared at me. "It's all their fault. Make them tell. Or they'll be sorry."

I stared at her, perplexed. "What can they tell? They weren't in the canoe with you."

"How can you be so dumb?" Sissy gave me a look of pure hatred. "Dulcie and Claire lied! They're *still* lying."

Emma looked from me to Sissy and back again. "What did Mommy lie about?"

"I was there," Sissy went on. "And so were they. I remember—and so do they!"

"Where were they?" Emma cried, her voice shrill with confusion and fear. "Tell me, Sissy, tell me!"

Sissy looked at me, not Emma. "Tell Dulcie what happened today." Each word dropped from her mouth, as hard as stone. "Don't leave anything out. Not the doll, not the canoe, not me. Then ask her what happened to Teresa."

"My mother and my aunt would never hurt anyone."

"No?" Sissy mocked me with her grin. "Oh, before I forget—make sure Dulcie knows the canoe belonged to your grandfather. He called it 'The Spirit of the Lake.' Good name, don't you think?"

Turning her back, Sissy swam away into the fog, taking the doll with her.

"Come back!" Emma cried after her. "You'll drown."

"You can't drown twice," Sissy called, her voice muffled by the water.

"Sissy," Emma called again. "Sissy!"

No one answered. No one came swimming out of the fog.

Emma clutched my arm. "Is Sissy really Sissy? Or is she somebody else?"

I hesitated, unsure how much she'd figured out. Finally, I said, "Deep down inside, I think you know who Sissy is."

Emma nodded slowly. "'You can't drown twice,'" she said, echoing Sissy's words.

I drew her closer to me, holding her tight. The water was cold, and our arms ached. I only hoped that someone would find us before we lost our grip on the canoe.

~18~

Just as daylight began to fade, a wind sprang up and blew the fog away, shred by shred. Not far off, I saw a motorboat headed in our direction.

"Help," I shouted, desperate to be seen. "Help, help!"

Emma yelled, too.

A man on the boat turned and looked in our direction. "There's two kids over there," he yelled to another man. "Hanging on to a canoe."

The boat turned and made its way toward Emma and me. In a few moments, strong hands pulled us out of the water and into the boat.

"Is your name Alison O'Dwyer?" the man asked.

"Yes, sir. And this is my cousin, Emma Madison. We—"

"It's the missing girls!" he shouted to his friend. "The ones we heard about on the radio. Call the harbor police. Let 'em know they're okay."

He wrapped us in blankets and poured hot tea from a thermos. Emma and I took the cups gratefully, warming our hands as we drank. I thought I'd never stop shivering.

"What the devil were you doing way out here?" he asked. "If the fog hadn't lifted when it did, we'd have passed right by and never seen you."

Emma burrowed into my side like a newborn kitten seeking warmth, leaving me to make up a credible story.

"We saw the canoe on the shore," I began, "and we thought it would be fun to try it out. But we didn't really know how to paddle, and we got lost in the fog. It was a stupid thing to do."

"It sure was," the man agreed. "The whole town's been looking for you two."

I squeezed Emma's hand, but neither of us said a word. We just huddled together under the scratchy wool blankets and watched as Webster's Cove came closer and closer.

At least half the town was waiting for us on the dock. As soon as the men tied the boat up, Dulcie ran to us. Her hair was a wild mass of uncombed curls, and she'd been crying. Sweeping up Emma, blanket and all, she held her tight. "Emma, Emma," she sobbed. "Thank God, you're safe."

I stood there, all alone. After what I'd been through, I needed comforting, too, but I had a sinking feeling I wouldn't get it from Dulcie. At any moment, I expected her to blame me for everything.

Suddenly, Ms. Trent was at my side, hugging me. "Ali, why didn't you wait for me? If anything had happened to you . . ." She hugged me again, even tighter.

Dulcie looked at me over Emma's head, as if she'd just remembered I was there. "*You* have some explaining to do," she said.

A policeman took her aside and began asking questions that I couldn't quite hear. Dulcie beckoned to me, and Ms. Trent squeezed my hand as if wishing me good luck. As my one friend disappeared into the crowd, Dulcie bundled Emma and me into the car.

"The police think you two should be checked at the emergency room," Dulcie said. Without looking at me, she secured Emma in her child safety seat and drove to the hospital.

A nurse led Emma and me to an examining room, where we stripped off our wet clothes and put on paper gowns about ten sizes too big for me and twenty sizes too big for Emma. Both of us were still shaking with cold.

A doctor examined us. She pronounced me fine, except for a touch of hypothermia, which would have been worse if we'd been in the water much longer. She said Emma was still running a fever, and might have strep throat as well as mild hypothermia.

"Continue with Emma's medicine," she told Dulcie. "Bundle them both up nice and warm, give them hot soup, hot tea, and plenty of love. They've had a terrible experience."

An hour or so later, I faced Dulcie across the kitchen table. By then, Emma was in bed, sound asleep.

Clutching her coffee mug in both hands, she seemed more unhappy than angry. In a way, that was worse. "Tell me why you took Emma out in that canoe," she said. "Without even a life jacket."

I fidgeted with my place mat as if it were vital to keep its edge parallel to the edge of the table. "Promise you won't be mad."

"Why shouldn't I be mad?"

I moved the place mat a bit to the right and then back to the left. "After you called Ms. Trent," I said in a low voice, "I left her house and went to look for Emma. I found her by the lake with Sissy. Sissy wanted to take her for a ride in an old canoe."

Watching Dulcie closely, I added, "It was called 'The Spirit of the Lake.' Sissy said it used to be Grandfather's canoe."

"Yes . . . that's what my father named it." Dulcie held the mug tightly, her whole body tense. "But it can't be the same canoe. He got rid of it after we stopped coming here."

"Sissy had that doll with her—the one you threw in the lake. She said if Emma got in the canoe, she could hold it. I tried to stop Emma, but she wouldn't listen to me. Finally, I got in, too." I shifted the place mat a fraction of an inch. "I didn't know what else to do."

Dulcie sat with her head in her hands. I couldn't see her face. "Go on," she said.

"Sissy paddled way out into the fog. We couldn't see the shore—we could hardly see each other. She started teasing Emma with the doll. And then she threw it in the water and the canoe turned over and . . ."

Dulcie got up and left the kitchen. She didn't look at me. She didn't say anything. She just walked out.

I stayed at the table, turning the place mat round and round aimlessly. Even though Dulcie had loaned me her warmest fleece bathrobe, I was still cold. Once I glanced at the window, fearing Sissy might be watching me, but the glass panes reflected the kitchen, hiding the darkness outside—as well as anything lurking there.

Finally, Dulcie came back. She sat down and shoved a photograph toward me. It was the same one I'd found at home, only it wasn't torn. There was Mom with a sad face, there was Dulcie beside her with a big grin, and there was the third girl, the one torn out of Mom's copy. Her face was almost hidden in the shadows, but her light hair caught the sunlight. Smirking with satisfaction, Sissy held the doll Edith, brand-new, her hair perfect.

Dulcie touched the photo with the tip of her finger. "That's Teresa Abbott, the girl who drowned in the lake."

To Dulcie, the girl was Teresa, but to Emma and me, she was Sissy. Even though I'd already figured it out, I shuddered.

Dulcie seized my hands and stared into my eyes. "Is Teresa . . . the girl you call Sissy?"

"Yes," I whispered.

"It can't be," Dulcie whispered. "It can't. I don't believe in ghosts, I don't *want* to believe in ghosts, but . . ." For a moment, she sat there speechless. "But there's no other explanation. Is there?"

I shook my head. Outside in the darkness, the wind rose, and something tapped the windowpane. I turned to look, expecting to see Sissy's face pressed against the glass, her thin fingers knocking to come in. But nothing was there.

Dulcie picked up her cup to drink, but her hands shook so badly she put it down without taking a sip. "It was the worst thing I ever did. I've tried to forget about it, pretend it never happened." Her voice dropped so low I could barely hear what she said. "But I can't forget her. And neither can your mother."

"Sissy doesn't want you to forget," I said.

Dulcie bent her head over the photo. "The doll," she said. "Edith. Mother gave it to Claire on her eighth birthday."

"But why is Sissy holding it?" I asked.

"Teresa loved to tease Claire with that doll. She'd snatch it way from her and make her beg to get it back. The more your mother cried, the more Teresa tormented her."

I stared at her, shocked. "You were the oldest. Why did you let Sissy pick on Mom like that?"

Dulcie studied the three girls in the photograph. "It's not a nice thing to say, but I used to be jealous of your mother," she said. "She was always sweet and nice, and I wasn't. Most people liked her better than me."

I wanted to sympathize with my aunt, but it hurt to learn that she let Sissy torment my mother. As an only child, I had all sorts of notions about sisters and how they took up for each other— blood being thicker than water and all that.

"So when Teresa teased Claire," Dulcie went on, "I'd go along with her. I guess I wanted her to like me more than Claire. Not a good excuse, but I'm afraid that's how it was." She looked past me, at the darkness outside. "Your mother was right. I should never have come back here."

I clung to the edge of my chair with both hands. "What happened the day Sissy drowned?"

Dulcie picked up the photo, put it down, turned it over to hide the three faces. "It was a few days after Claire's birthday," she began. "Mom and Dad had gone shopping in Webster's Cove. Teresa came over and started teasing Claire. She grabbed Edith and ran down the steps to the lake. I dashed after her, laughing. Claire followed me, crying for the doll."

She paused to take a sip of coffee, made a face, and put the mug down. "Cold."

"What happened next?" I asked.

"Teresa got in Dad's canoe," Dulcie said. "It was against the rules to go anywhere in that canoe without one of our parents, but I jumped in after her."

Dulcie shook her head. "But not Claire. Even then she was scared of water. She stood on the dock, threatening to tell. Teresa said if Claire didn't come with us, she'd take Edith home and keep her."

The wind had picked up, and it moaned in the pines the way it had in the cemetery. It seemed as if all the sadness in the world had been sucked up into that sound.

"Claire finally got in the canoe," Dulcie went on, "and Teresa pushed off. We hadn't gotten very far when the fog rolled in. We couldn't see the shore. It was like being lost in a cloud. Kind of magical and scary at the same time."

She started pacing around the kitchen. "Teresa tossed Edith to me. I threw her to Teresa. Claire lunged back and forth, rocking the canoe, trying to catch her doll. A game of keep-away—that's how it started. Kids play it all the time. But it wasn't a game to Claire. She begged me to give her the doll. She kept saying, 'You're my sister, Dulcie, you're my sister!'"

Dulcie stopped pacing and poured herself more coffee, hot this time. "Suddenly, I got sick of the whole thing. Sick of Teresa. Sick of Claire. Sick of the stupid doll. When Teresa tossed it to me, I threw it in the lake. I grabbed the paddle from Teresa and started to turn around. I figured that was the end of it: *Nobody* would have the doll."

She went to the window and peered out into the windy night. "But things didn't go the way I planned. Claire sat there crying, like she always did, but Teresa was stubborn. She wanted that doll so badly she jumped into the lake after it. The canoe tipped over then, and Claire and I went in, too. I got Claire to the canoe, and we hung on to the sides. But Teresa swam after the doll. I yelled at her to come back. She ignored me. And then she was gone. Just like that. In the water with us one minute, lost in the fog the next. Claire and I shouted till we were hoarse, but Teresa didn't answer."

I watched my aunt go from one window to the next as if she were still looking for Teresa. "The canoe floated to shore, where the rocks are. We left it there and ran all the way home. I told Claire it was a trick. Teresa had fooled us somehow. She'd be waiting for us on the porch. I think I believed it myself." Dulcie glanced at me. "But she wasn't there."

She picked up a sponge and wiped away a spot on the counter.

"Claire started crying again. So did I. Teresa was dead—we knew she was. And it was my fault. I'd thrown the doll in the lake. I thought I'd be charged with murder, arrested, sent to jail. I was just a child—what did I know about the law, or what could happen to me?" Her voice rose. She was breathing hard, talking fast, as if the police might arrive at any moment, sirens howling, lights flashing.

"I made Claire promise not to tell anyone we'd gone out in the canoe. We'd been in the house all day. We hadn't seen Teresa."

Dulcie sat down across from me. "When our parents came home, we were sitting right here at the kitchen table, drawing pictures, doing our best to act like nothing was wrong. A few minutes later, the phone rang. It was Mrs. Abbott. Mom turned to us and asked if we'd seen Teresa. We lied and said no. After that, we couldn't stop lying. We lied to the Abbotts, to the police, to everyone. Even ourselves. It was horrible. Horrible. I didn't mean for Teresa to die, I didn't—it was an accident."

Dulcie covered her face with her hands and began to cry. "I'd give anything to go back in time and undo what I did."

I sat there, a silent lump of misery, too shocked to say anything. My mother and my aunt had lied. *Lied.* And all these years, they'd gone on lying. And Sissy had lain alone in the lake, waiting for them to come back. Waiting for them to tell the truth.

Finally, Dulcie reached for the tissue box. Her face was pale, her eyes red rimmed and puffy.

"What are you going to do?" I asked.

"Go back to New York." She blew her nose. "We'll leave tomorrow."

"But what about Sissy?"

"Sissy?" Dulcie stared at me as if I'd lost my mind.

"Teresa, I mean." It was hard to call Sissy anything but Sissy. "I told you what she said. You have to tell the truth—or you'll be sorry."

Dulcie jumped up and went to the window again. The glass streamed with rain. "Who can I tell? Mr. and Mrs. Abbott are dead. I don't know where her sister, Linda, is."

I followed my aunt and rested my head against her shoulder. "How about the police?"

"They wouldn't be interested after all these years." Dulcie peered into the rainy night. "Besides, it was an accident. I didn't know Teresa would jump out of the canoe. I didn't know she'd drown." Her voice wavered and grew stronger. "I was scared. For God's sake, I was only ten years old!"

Tippety-tap, tippety-tap. The branch whipped back and forth in the wind, rapping against the glass again.

Suddenly, Dulcie closed the curtains and moved away from the window. "I can't talk about this," she said. "I'm going to bed."

I watched her walk toward Emma's room. I stayed where I was, my back to the window. A few moments later, Dulcie carried Emma down the hall to her bedroom. Emma was sound asleep, limp and relaxed in her mother's arms. Dulcie didn't look at me or say anything. In the silence, I heard the door close behind them.

Reluctantly, I climbed the stairs to my room. Never had I felt so sad or so totally and completely alone. Why hadn't Dulcie invited me to sleep with her and Emma? Didn't she think I needed company, too?

At the top of the steps, a cold draft rushed out to meet me, circling my ankles, chilling me from the knees down. My window was wide open, and the rain had blown inside, soaking the floor and the magazines on top of my bookcase. I rushed to the casement and struggled with the crank, fighting the wind to close it.

As I reached for the light, a cold hand grabbed my wrist. "Don't bother," Sissy whispered. "I'm used to the dark." In her other hand, she clutched Edith the doll.

More startled than scared, I tried to pull away from her, but she held me tightly. The doll fell to the floor as we struggled. "What do you want?" I whispered.

"Did you tell Dulcie what happened today?"

"Yes." I peered at Sissy's thin, pointed face. "And she told me what happened to you."

Sissy kept her icy grip on my wrist. "So she remembers after all. Is she going to confess what she did?"

"It was an accident, Sissy," I said slowly. "Dulcie didn't mean for you to drown. She didn't push you in the lake—you jumped."

Sissy tightened her hold on my wrist and scowled. "She knew I'd go after the doll. She hated me—just like you do. She planned the whole thing. She wanted me to drown."

I heard the anger in her voice, and I saw the anguish in her eyes. "Dulcie didn't want you to die," I said. "She didn't hate you. And neither do I."

Sissy let go of me and rescued Edith from a puddle of rainwater on the floor. "You used to hate me," she muttered, hugging the doll to her skinny chest. "Now you just feel sorry for me. You don't really like me. Nobody does."

I rubbed my wrist to take the chill of Sissy's hands away. She stood by the window, holding the doll tightly, her face filled with misery.

"You're cold." I took a spare blanket from the closet and wrapped it around her. Then I dried her hair with a T-shirt, rubbing her scalp hard to warm her. It was strange—she felt solid but somehow insubstantial, boneless, as if she could melt away at any moment.

"Will you comb my hair?" she asked.

I sat her down on the edge of the bed and worked a comb through her tangles. No one had done anything about her hair for a long time. But even though I was sure I must be hurting her, she sat still and didn't complain.

When her hair was smooth, she ran her fingers through it. Allowing herself a small smile, she said, "Prove you don't hate me. Let me sleep in your bed tonight. I'm so tired of the dark and the cold."

I got into bed and reluctantly let Sissy curl up beside me. It was like lying next to a snow girl made on the coldest night of winter.

"Are you scared," she whispered, "to share your bed with me?"

"You're just a little girl," I said.

"Not an ordinary one."

"No, not ordinary. Not ordinary at all."

Sissy sat halfway up. "Do you know what I am?"

"Yes, I know."

"Did you suspect all along?"

"No. You seemed like a real girl, not a—"

"Shh." She pressed her cold hand against my mouth. "Don't say it. I hate that word."

"I didn't guess till I saw the sweatshirt in the angel's hand," I said. "And read your name on the stone."

She leaned over me, and I smelled the lake on her breath. Not exactly fresh, a bit musty, a little earthy. "Make Dulcie tell—not just you, but everybody. I've been waiting a long time for her to come back."

With that, she lay down again, a small hump under the covers, not quite as cold as she'd been before.

Too tense to sleep, I lay beside her, staring into the darkness. Dulcie *had* to tell the truth. Not just for Sissy's sake but for her own. And Mom's, too. Otherwise, none of them would ever be at peace.

19

In the morning, Sissy was gone. And so was the wind and the rain. The sky was a brilliant blue, and the air smelled like honeysuckle and roses. I lay still for a moment, wishing the world was as ordinary as it seemed. Sun shining, birds singing, no dark shadows, no secrets, no lies.

Downstairs, Emma was chattering away to her mother as if nothing had happened yesterday. If only that were true.

I pulled on shorts and a T-shirt and headed for the kitchen. Dulcie looked up from the stove. "Emma's feeling much better today," she said, trying hard to sound cheerful. "Her fever's gone, and she wants pancakes."

I sat down and stared at the plate Dulcie set in front of me. I wasn't hungry, but I didn't want to hurt my aunt's feelings. She wasn't often inspired to cook a real breakfast.

"Last night," I started to say but stopped myself. Why bring up Sissy? Dulcie's smile might change to a frown. Emma's laughter might change to tears.

"Last night," I told Dulcie, "I dreamed you fixed pancakes for breakfast, and you made so many it took us till Christmas to eat them all."

Emma laughed so hard, maple syrup dribbled out of her mouth and ran down her chin. That made Dulcie and me laugh.

After we'd eaten, Emma got out her drawing tablet and busied herself making a picture with black, purple, and blue crayons. All scribbles, very dark.

Dulcie drew me aside, signaling that Emma mustn't hear. "I've made an appointment to see a lawyer in Webster's Cove today. My parents knew him. I'll talk to him about Teresa's death."

"Do you want me to come with you?"

"Not to the lawyer's. I thought you and Emma might enjoy browsing in shops, getting ice cream, strolling along the boardwalk." Dulcie glanced at Emma, who was still bent over her picture, totally absorbed. "She needs a day out. And so do you."

"Hey, Em," I called. "Better get dressed. We're going to town."

Emma laid her crayons down and ran to her room. While she was gone, Dulcie and I took a quick look at her picture. Dark and scribbly as it was, we could both make out a boat with two girls in it. A third girl was in the water, along with Edith the doll.

Cars crowded Webster's Cove's narrow streets, and vacationers thronged the boardwalk and the beach. Like me, they'd been here long enough to value sunshine, blue water, and warm air. It had rained yesterday and the day before, and most likely it would rain again tomorrow and the day after.

Dulcie left us at Smoochie's, telling Emma she had a few errands to run. "I'll meet you here at noon, and we'll have lunch somewhere."

Erin was busy scooping ice cream for three teenagers. When she'd finished, she smiled at Emma and me. "Long time no see. Where have you two been?"

"Playing at our beach," Emma said.

"With that girl Sissy?" Erin asked.

Emma toyed with the candy and gum display beside the cash register. "Sissy's gone, I think."

"Hey, Em," I said. "They have tutti-frutti today. It's yummy."

Erin held up a little white paper cup, the kind you use to rinse your mouth at the dentist's. "How about a sample?"

Emma took the cup, stuck her tongue into the ice cream, thought a moment, and handed it back. "Can I have chocolate instead? That's my most favorite kind of all."

While Erin packed two scoops of chocolate into a cone, Emma stood in the doorway and watched people stroll past. A display of faded Smoochie's T-shirts swayed in the breeze over her head. Such an ordinary day, such ordinary people. I wondered if any of them had ever seen a ghost. Would they believe me if I told them about Sissy?

Erin handed me Emma's cone. "What kind do you want?"

"Tutti-frutti, of course." With images of Sissy crowding my head, I felt like an actress playing the part of a normal girl.

Erin bent over the ice cream and struggled to fill the scoop. "It's always hard as a rock in the morning. By afternoon, it'll be like soup."

"Is that mine?" Emma reached for the chocolate cone. I gave it to her, and she wandered back to the door.

Erin went on scooping, her head down. "My mother told me she visited your aunt, but she said she wasn't very friendly. Your aunt got all bent out of shape when Mom mentioned Teresa Abbott."

"Dulcie didn't mean to be rude," I said. "She just doesn't like to talk about Teresa."

Erin straightened up and wiped her hands on her apron. "So she *does* remember. Mom thought she'd repressed the whole thing. Either that or she was lying." She handed me my cone. "It must have been awful for her and your mom."

"It was." I paid Erin for the cones and followed Emma outside. Like Dulcie, I had no desire to discuss Teresa Abbott with anyone. She was our secret, a dark little shadow at the edge of the real world.

Emma and I sat on the boardwalk and ate our ice cream, slurping it down before it melted. Some teenagers were playing volleyball on the sand. We watched them shout and laugh and jump around, cheering each other on. Their voices blended with the cries of gulls and the *wish, wash* of the lake's little waves.

Down by the water's edge, a man threw a Frisbee out over the lake. His dog, a big black Lab with a red kerchief tied around his neck, splashed into the water after it. He ran out of the lake with the Frisbee in his mouth and shook so much water from his coat that a woman complained to his owner.

I wished Emma and I were down by the water playing with the dog, happy, having fun, like girls on a vacation.

Suddenly, Emma turned her chocolate-smeared face to me. "Did Mommy really push Sissy in the water?"

"No. She got mad and threw the doll into the lake, and Sissy went after it. It was foggy, like yesterday, and Dulcie and Mom couldn't find her. The canoe drifted, and they washed up on the rocks. They went home and lied to everyone because they were scared it was their fault that Sissy drowned."

"Poor Sissy." Emma edged closer to me. "Mommy and Aunt Claire shouldn't have lied."

"I think they know that now."

Side by side, we gazed at the lake, blue and calm under a cloudless sky. Children Emma's age darted in and out of the water, shrieking and splashing each other. The teenagers laughed and shouted, and the volleyball flew back and forth across the net. The dog fetched the Frisbee again and again, never tiring of the game. It seemed everyone was happy but us.

"Do you want to wade in the water?" I asked Emma. "Or build castles in the sand?"

She shook her head, and we stayed where we were.

By the time Dulcie joined us, I'd braided Emma's hair into two short plaits and tied them with a piece of string. They were a little crooked, but Emma liked them. She tossed her head back and forth to show them to her mother.

"Very cute." Dulcie eyed Emma's T-shirt, face, and hands. "It looks like you really enjoyed your ice cream. Chocolate, huh?"

Emma smiled and took her mother's hand. We walked along the boardwalk to a little restaurant with a deck built out over the lake and seated ourselves at a table shaded by a green umbrella. Dulcie and I ordered lobster rolls and iced tea, but Emma asked for chocolate milk and a hamburger. Just plain, she said, no lettuce, no tomato, no pickle. But with French fries and lots of ketchup.

The waitress—a college girl, I guessed—smiled at Emma. "I love a kid who knows exactly what she wants."

While we waited for our food, Dulcie gave Emma a few slices of bread from a basket on the table. "Why don't you go feed the gulls?"

Emma ran to the railing and began tossing bits of bread into the air. In seconds, she was surrounded by dozens of hungry gulls, screaming for their share.

Dulcie turned to me. "I told Mr. Goldsmith the whole story," she began, "leaving out Sissy, of course. He said it's pointless to go to the police now. The case was closed years ago. Accidental drowning." She took a sip of water. "He told me Claire and I weren't—aren't—responsible for Teresa's death. Even if we'd told the truth the day it happened, it wouldn't have changed anything."

"What does he think you should do?"

"Forget about it." She gave me a bitter smile. "If only it were that easy."

I thought of Sissy begging me to make Dulcie tell the truth, to take some of the blame for what happened. "But you can't just forget about it, you have to tell—"

Dulcie laid her hand on mine. "I know, Ali. Believe me, I know." She turned her head to watch Emma hurl the last of the bread to the gulls. "I'm going to talk to someone at *The Sentinel* after lunch. It's the kind of story newspapers love." Her hand tightened on mine. "Will your mother be upset?"

"I think she'll be okay with it," I said, hoping I was right.

"Here you are." The waitress set our food on the table, and Emma came running.

"Did you see me feeding the gulls?" she asked the girl.

"I sure did. You must have fed the entire population."

"They're big," Emma said, "and they have sharp beaks and mean yellow eyes, but I wasn't scared."

"I bet nothing scares you." The waitress stood with her empty tray pressed to her chest, smiling down at Emma.

"Sometimes nothing is the scariest thing of all," Emma said in a low voice, but the waitress had already turned her attention to a family at another table. No one heard her but me.

After we'd eaten, Dulcie told us she had one more thing to do before we went home. "How about you and Ali waiting for me at the arcade?" she asked Emma. "You can ride the carousel, the

Ferris wheel, the bumper cars—anything but the Tilt-A-Whirl. You'll throw up for sure on that one."

Emma clapped her hands with pleasure, too excited to notice that Dulcie had eaten less than half of her lobster roll. She'd barely touched her French fries. And she hadn't even bothered to taste the coffee she'd ordered instead of dessert. I watched her walk away, head down, shoulders slumped. If I hadn't known she was doing the right thing, I would have run after her and stopped her.

In a hurry to get to the carousel at the end of the boardwalk, Emma ran ahead, towing me along behind her. Soon she was perched on a fancy white horse wearing a garland of carved flowers, and I was beside her on a black horse. We went up and down and round and round, accompanied by old-fashioned organ music. I smelled popcorn and cotton candy and suntan oil.

Emma seemed as happy as the other children. She laughed and waved to everyone, and they waved back. It amazed me that her mood could change so quickly. Here I was, worrying about Dulcie, brooding about Sissy, wanting my mother, and there Emma was, the princess of the carousel.

By the time Dulcie came back, we'd ridden the carousel five times, the Ferris wheel once, and the bumper cars twice. We'd also eaten cotton candy and shared a box of popcorn. We were ready to go home.

At the car, Dulcie fumbled with the buckle on Emma's safety belt. "Sit still," she said, her voice sharp. "How do you expect me to do this with you wiggling like that?"

Emma frowned. "I'm not wiggling."

"There." Dulcie snapped the buckle, slammed the back door, and got into the front seat beside me.

With a jerk, she pulled away from the curb and headed into the afternoon traffic. "I hate tourists," she muttered. "Why do they have to come here and ruin everything? Crowds, trash everywhere. It's a disgrace."

Her change of mood told me things hadn't gone well at *The Sentinel.*

Not long after we got home, Emma fell sound asleep on the couch, worn out from all the excitement. Afternoon sunlight washed the walls with pale yellow, and a calm stillness filled the house.

I joined Dulcie on the deck. "They're running the story next week," she said. "A photographer's coming on Sunday to shoot some pictures. They want to talk to the police as well, and some of the other people who remember Teresa and her family."

Getting to her feet, she walked to the railing and stared at the lake. "The way they acted, you'd think I just confessed to murder. I should have gone back to New York and never said a thing about this. Or never come here at all. What was I thinking anyway?"

"Are you going to call Mom?" I asked. "And tell her?"

Dulcie looked over her shoulder at me. "Do you think I should?"

"She might want to come."

"Yes, I guess she might." Dulcie went to the door.

I followed her inside. "Can I talk to her, too?"

"Of course." Dulcie picked up the receiver and dialed our number. I heard Mom answer. In a low voice, Dulcie told her what she'd done. "I thought you'd want to be here. If we get this out in the open, maybe we can put it behind us."

From where I stood, next to Dulcie, I heard Mom crying into

the phone. "Yes," she sobbed. "Yes, I'll come. Pete and I can drive up Saturday."

"Thanks, Claire. . . . Ali wants to talk to you." Dulcie handed me the receiver.

"Are you okay?" Mom asked. The worry in her voice surged through the line.

"Yes, I'm fine."

"Dulcie shouldn't have told you."

"She had to tell the truth," I said.

In the silence before Mom spoke, I heard a familiar whisper. "Tell her about me. Let her know I'm still here. Just like she thought."

Sissy stood a few feet away where the shadows were darkest, holding the doll and frowning. "If you don't tell her, I will." With that, she vanished without a sound, unseen and unheard by anyone but me.

"Did you say something?" Mom asked.

"No," I stammered. "It's just Emma, playing with her paper dolls."

"I thought I heard . . ." For a moment or two, Mom breathed slowly into the phone as if she were trying to calm herself. At last she said, "Do you hate Dulcie and me for leaving Teresa to drown?"

The question took me by surprise. "Of course not, Mom. You tried to find her, you—"

She broke in. "Maybe if we'd tried harder, we could have saved her. If we'd told someone right away. If we'd—" She started crying. "I go over it again and again. I can't stop thinking about Teresa, about leaving her there—it's haunted me my whole life."

"It wasn't your fault. You were just a little kid, you didn't throw the doll, you—"

Dulcie had crossed the room and now snatched the phone from my hand. "Stop it, Claire," she said to my mother. "What happened, happened. Nothing can change that. You'll just have to deal with it."

I reached for the phone, but Dulcie shook her head. "Go see what Emma's doing. I'll say goodbye to your mother for you."

I retreated to the living room and tried to listen to Dulcie's end of the conversation. It sounded as if she was bullying Mom, talking tough, acting the part of big sister. Silently, I egged Mom on. *Stand up for yourself, stop crying, tell her you're an adult, too.* By the time Dulcie hung up, I was beginning to wonder if I'd ever look up to my aunt the way I used to.

Fearing she'd know I'd been eavesdropping, I sat down quickly on the sofa next to Emma. She woke up just as Dulcie entered the room, clutching a cup of coffee—her fifth, sixth? It was hard to keep count. Her blood must've been pure caffeine.

She stood by the window, looking out at the lake, ignoring both of us. Her back was tense, rigid almost. "Is your mother still seeing a shrink?" she asked.

"She's depressed," I said. "She tries not to be, but—"

Dulcie spun around and faced me. "Don't tell me about depression. She needs something to do besides moon over her flowers. She used to write poetry, she used to draw. Now she just sits around feeling sorry for herself."

"It wouldn't kill you to be nicer to her." Fed up with Dulcie, I left the house. Ignoring Emma's call to wait for her, I ran down the steps to the lake. I needed some time alone. No Emma, no Dulcie, no Sissy—*especially* no Sissy. If I saw her, I'd run.

I walked all the way back to Webster's Cove and treated

myself to ice cream. But I was still in a bad mood when I returned. Worse in a way, because I was now tired and hot.

Somehow I got through dinner without making a scene and managed to read to Emma before bedtime. Dulcie had nothing much to say—which was fine with me. An apology was all I wanted to hear from her, but I had a feeling that was not going to happen. While I read to Emma, my aunt sat in one of the old armchairs, drinking yet another cup of coffee. She'd pulled her hair up into an untidy topknot, and her hands and arms were streaked with the same black paint that spattered her jeans and T-shirt.

Sitting around feeling sorry for yourself. Isn't that what you accused Mom of doing? I thought.

"Bedtime." Dulcie roused herself to pick up Emma.

"I want to hear another chapter!"

"I'm tired, and so are you, and so is Ali. It's time we all went to bed."

Without another word, not even "Good night," Dulcie carried Emma off to bed. I guessed that meant she was just as mad with me as I was with her.

When I went up to my room, I found Sissy perched on my bed, holding Edith on her lap. I wasn't surprised to see her. It was obvious she wasn't done with us.

"Did Dulcie tell the truth at last?" she asked.

"She talked to her lawyer. He said she hadn't committed a crime. And then he told her she should forget the whole thing."

Sissy sneered. "She's been doing a pretty good job of that all along."

I bristled. "Dulcie's never forgotten a single detail of that day. Neither has Mom. In fact, Mom feels worse than Dulcie. In a way, it's ruined her whole life."

"How about me? Don't you think they ruined *my* life?" Sissy asked plaintively. "Believe me, I feel a whole lot worse than either of them!"

"I'm sorry," I said. "It was stupid of me to say that."

"Yes, it was," Sissy agreed, clearly pleased I'd apologized.

"After she saw her lawyer," I went on, "Dulcie talked to a reporter at *The Sentinel*. A photographer's coming here to take pictures, and they're going to interview lots of people, including Dulcie and my mother."

Sissy smiled a real smile for once. "That's just exactly what I wanted. Everybody in Webster's Cove will know the truth at last."

She watched me get ready for bed, and then crawled in beside me. Shivering, I moved toward the wall, giving her as much room as I could.

"Just a few more nights," she whispered, "and then you'll never see me again."

Once I would've been happy to hear that, but tonight I felt an unexpected twinge of sadness. Odd as it sounds, I was getting used to having Sissy around. Now that I knew so much more about her, it was easier to put up with her sadness and anger.

~20~

In the morning, Sissy was gone, but her pillow was damp and cold.

Dulcie met me at the foot of the steps. She'd tidied her hair, washed off the paint, and changed her clothes, but she was still tense and edgy. Behind her, I could see Emma sitting at the kitchen table, coloring a picture.

I looked at my aunt warily, braced for another outburst.

Glancing at Emma, she spoke in a low voice, "I'm sorry for my behavior yesterday. I was upset. And Claire just fell apart. I needed her to be strong, so I could be strong." She reached out to hug me, and I felt myself begin to relax.

"I never should have criticized your mother," Dulcie said. "She can't help being depressed. I know she's trying to get better. Please forgive me, Ali. I love you both, your mother and you. We're all the family we have."

I returned her hug. "It's okay, I understand." *That is, I think I do.*

Dulcie let me go and gazed at me thoughtfully. "Did you tell your mother about Teresa?"

"You mean, Sissy? No," I said. "But even if we don't say a word, Sissy will figure out a way to let her know."

"You really saw her?" Dulcie whispered. "It wasn't a kid playing a trick?"

"It was her," I said. "Teresa . . . Sissy . . . whatever you want to call her. She's been hanging around all summer."

Dulcie shook her head. "I'm sorry, Ali, but that's hard to believe, especially on a sunny day like this."

A little later, I heard a car. Although it was way too early to be Mom and Dad, I ran to the door.

Ms. Trent got out of her faded blue Volvo and waved to me. "I was driving past, and I thought I'd drop in. Is your aunt here?"

I beckoned her to follow me inside. "Ms. Trent's come to see you," I told Dulcie.

She looked up from the newspaper and made an effort to smile. "I just made a fresh pot of coffee. Would you like a cup?"

"I never turn one down." Ms. Trent followed Dulcie to the kitchen. I heard her say something in a low voice.

Dulcie turned to me. "Weren't you going to make paper dolls for Emma?"

"Yes, yes, you promised!" Emma grabbed my hand and towed me out to the deck. She'd left paper, crayons, and scissors scattered across the picnic table. "Make one like you and one like me and one like—" She stopped. "No, just make two. You and me. Best friends."

Emma watched me draw, her face so close I could feel her warm breath on my hand. While she chattered on about the clothes she wanted for her doll, I strained to hear Dulcie and Ms. Trent's conversation. I picked up a word here, a word there, enough to know they were talking about Teresa. Or Sissy. Whichever she preferred to be called.

Emma jumped up suddenly. "There's a cat. It's after a bird!"

A big black and white cat was creeping across the grass, belly to the ground, eyes on a sparrow that was pecking at seeds spilled from the bird feeder.

When Emma ran across the lawn to stop it, I moved closer to the kitchen window, hoping to hear better.

"Nothing's a secret in Webster's Cove," Ms. Trent was saying. "Ed Jones, the reporter you talked to, has a wife with a big mouth. She called Jeanine Donaldson and told her the whole story. Jeanine didn't waste a second spreading the news. By the time she told me, the whole town knew, including Teresa's sister, who lives a few miles away in Lakeport—which was news to me."

"Ali, come help me!" I turned to see Emma holding the small brown bird in her hands. "It's still alive."

While the cat watched from the bushes, I ran to Emma's side. The sparrow flapped its wings feebly. Its yellow beak opened and closed slowly. While I watched, its eyes lost their luster, and it stopped moving.

"Can we save it?" Emma asked.

I took the sparrow from her as gently as I could. "The poor little thing," I whispered. "It's dead."

Emma began to cry. "I hate cats. I hate them!"

The old stray lurked under the bush, twitching its tail. It was clear it felt no remorse. Given the opportunity, the cat would have snatched the bird and run off with it.

Emma bent down to pick up a stone. Before she could throw it, I grabbed her arm. "No," I said. "Cats can't help killing things. It's their nature."

Emma dropped the stone and touched the bird's body sadly. "Can we bury it?"

I went inside to find a large spoon to dig a grave, and Emma followed me, still crying for the bird. "Why do things have to

161

die?" she cried, burrowing into her mother's arms. "It's not fair."

I showed the dead sparrow to Dulcie and Ms. Trent. "A cat killed it. We're going to bury it."

"Do birds have ghosts?" Emma asked Dulcie.

Over Emma's head, Dulcie and Ms. Trent glanced at each other. Ms. Trent shook her head, and Dulcie said, "Of course not, darling. There's no—"

Emma straightened up and looked Dulcie in the eye. "Don't say there's no such thing. Ghosts are real. You know it, and I know it, and Ali knows it." She hesitated a second. "And *Sissy* knows it."

Emma stood there gazing at her mother, daring her to argue.

"We came in to get a spoon," I told Dulcie, "so we can dig a grave for the bird."

While Dulcie selected an appropriate spoon, I ran to my room for a tissue box I'd thrown in the trash that morning. We wrapped the bird in an old handkerchief and laid it in the box. Then Emma and I took turns digging a hole under a lilac bush, and gently placed the box in the ground.

While we said a few words over the bird, I felt my neck prickle, as if someone was watching us. Uneasily, I glanced over my shoulder. Almost hidden in the shade of a tall oak, Sissy peered at me. When she realized I'd seen her, she ducked out of sight.

I returned my attention to the pile of earth heaped beside the small grave and spooned some onto the box. Emma followed my example. With Dulcie and Ms. Trent helping, we filled the hole and tamped it down firmly to keep the cat from digging up its victim.

Before we returned to the house, I looked at the oak tree. Sissy was gone.

Dulcie filled two coffee mugs for herself and Ms. Trent and poured lemonade for Emma and me. While my aunt and Ms. Trent sat at the table, they chatted quietly about quilting and painting. Ms. Trent said a small gallery had just opened on the main road. Dulcie asked about an arts and crafts shop she'd noticed on a side street. They both deplored the crowded roads and beach. It was comforting to hear them talk about ordinary things.

After Ms. Trent left, I sat on the deck, watching for Dad's car. It was almost five thirty. The sky had clouded over, promising rain once more, and daylight was already fading. Inside, Dulcie was preparing a special seafood dinner, and Emma was playing with the paper dolls I'd made.

Dulcie came to the window and looked at me. "It's about to rain," she called. "Aren't you cold?"

I shook my head. "It's nice out here."

Dulcie shrugged. "Suit yourself."

As she turned away, I heard a car coming toward the house. I jumped up and ran to meet my parents as if we'd been apart for years instead of weeks. I hugged Dad tight and then threw my arms around Mom. She cried, wetting my face with tears, and turned to Dulcie.

"I never thought I'd see this place again." Mom looked around, her face worried. "It's just as I remembered. Nothing's changed."

"Except us," Dulcie threw her arms around Mom. "It's good to see you, Claire."

As she hugged Dad, I glanced at the oak tree. Sissy watched from the shadows, her pale face expressionless.

Emma saw her, too. I grabbed her arm to stop her from running to meet her, but I needn't have bothered. Sissy was already gone.

"Why did she run away?" Emma whispered. "Is she still mad?"

"It's got nothing to do with you and me," I told her. "Sissy wants to see our mothers. But she doesn't want them to see her."

Taking her hand, I led my cousin into the house. For once, she didn't argue.

While the adults chatted, Emma and I set the table for dinner. No one mentioned Teresa Abbott—not then and not during dinner. Emma and I talked about swimming and drawing and Webster's Cove. We complained about the rain and the fog and the mosquitoes, and my parents complained about the heat and humidity at home.

Mom told me the kid next door had broken his ankle skateboarding. My friend Julie got a hideous permanent and was threatening to shave her head. Mrs. Burgess had named her new baby girl Meadow, of all things. We laughed and talked and enjoyed the flounder-and-scallops extravaganza that Dulcie had invented.

After we'd cleared the table and washed the dishes, Dad built a fire. Dulcie produced marshmallows for Emma and me to toast. It had begun to rain while we were eating, and it was coming down harder now. The wind had risen, too. Thunder boomed, and lightning flashed. Emma and I abandoned the marshmallows and curled up with our parents.

"I hate storms," Mom said.

"I love them—the wilder and fiercer, the better!" Dulcie jumped to her feet and ran to a window to watch the lightning. I wondered if she were putting on an act for Mom, striking a pose, trying to convince us she was fearless. She didn't fool me. I knew her too well now, maybe even better than Mom did.

"Come away from the window," Mom pleaded. "Lightning might strike you."

Dulcie laughed. "Don't be silly, Claire. The chances of that are a billion to one."

Emma ran to her mother and tugged at her hand. "Sit on the couch with me, Mommy."

Suddenly, Dulcie gasped and backed away from the window.

"What did you see?" Emma pressed her face to the glass. "Is it Sissy?"

Dulcie ran her hands through her hair, tugging it back from her face. "Come away, Emma. No one's there."

"Sissy," Emma persisted. "Sissy's out there." She pressed her face against the glass and peered into the rain.

Mom looked up from her magazine, her face anxious. "Was someone at the window?"

"Of course not," Dad said quickly. "Who'd be out in a storm like this?"

I could have said, *Someone who doesn't mind being wet.* But I didn't.

"Who was it?" Mom asked Dulcie. "Don't lie. Tell me, tell me now!"

Alarmed by her rising voice, Dad moved closer to her. "No one was there, Claire."

Mom ignored him. Her attention was fixed on her sister and the window behind her. "It was her, wasn't it?"

"Calm down, Claire," Dad begged. "Breathe slowly, deeply. Relax. You'll give yourself a headache if you get upset."

Dulcie stayed by the window, holding Emma tightly. "Do you really want to know?" she asked Mom. Her voice was calm, but her face was flushed, her eyes bright as if she had a fever.

Dad looked from Dulcie to Mom and back to Dulcie. "What kind of game are you playing now?"

"No game." Dulcie smoothed Emma's hair. "I grew out of games a long time ago."

Emma squirmed free of her mother and ran to Mom. "Don't worry. Sissy won't hurt you. She just wants to see what you look like now."

Mom shuddered and drew back. "Sissy?"

"Teresa," Dulcie said. "She's been calling herself Sissy. The girls have seen her, played with her." She hesitated a moment. "They even went out in the canoe with her."

Mom looked at me, pale and wide-eyed, like someone waking from a nightmare and finding it's not a dream after all. "You *saw* Teresa? You got in a *canoe* with her?" Shaking with anger, she turned to her sister. "Oh, Dulcie, Dulcie, how could you let them do it? I knew you wouldn't watch them. I knew it!"

"If you'd been here instead of moping in Maryland, afraid of everything—"

Emma spoke up loudly enough to get her mother's attention. "Sissy showed us how Mommy threw Edith in the water." To demonstrate, she made a throwing motion. "She wanted me to get Edith, but she fell in, too. I thought she was going to drown all over again. And then the canoe got upset and I was afraid me and Ali would drown."

Mom gasped and leaned against Dad's side. For a second, I thought she was going to faint. "See what you've done?" she asked Dulcie. "You've brought it all back. Why couldn't you have let things be?"

"So you could have headaches all your life?" Dulcie asked bitterly.

I squeezed onto the sofa beside Mom and clasped her hands in mine. "Don't you see? Dulcie *had* to come here. She had to tell the truth so Sissy—Teresa—"

"Don't say her name." Mom started crying. "I can't bear to hear it."

"Sissy won't hurt you, Aunt Claire." Emma climbed into Mom's lap and wrapped her arms around her. "She just wants you and Mommy to tell what really happened."

Dulcie gently pulled Emma away from Mom. "That's enough, sweetie," she said softly. "It's time for bed."

Emma started to protest, but the look on her mother's face silenced her. Meekly, she let Dulcie carry her out of the room.

Dad looked at Mom as if he feared she was hallucinating. "What are you so upset about, Claire? You told me Teresa drowned years ago. How can she be here now?"

Mom didn't answer. She was watching the window as if she expected to see Sissy's face.

Turning to me, Dad said, "Can you please tell me what's going on?"

Before I could answer, Mom pressed her fingers to her temples and said, "I can't stay here a minute longer, Pete. Please take Ali and me to Webster's Cove. Find a motel, a bed-and-breakfast, whatever. I'll sleep in the car if I have to—any place but this cottage."

Dad stared at her, shocked. "We can't walk out on your sister. What will she think?"

"My head aches so badly, I don't care what anyone thinks, least of all Dulcie," Mom said. "I'll lose my mind if I don't get out of here."

"I don't understand," Dad said. "What *is* it about this cottage? You'd think it was haunted or something—"

"It *is* haunted," I said. "Weren't you listening to what we said?"

"That's crazy, absolutely crazy," Dad said. "I thought you had more sense, Ali." Giving me an annoyed look, he went to the door and peered into the darkness as if he expected to see a little girl outside—a real little girl who'd laugh and admit she'd played a trick on us. Of course, he saw no one.

Shaking his head, he sat down beside Mom again. "It's a hoax," he said. "Someone with a grudge is behind the whole thing. Maybe Teresa has relatives who blame Dulcie and you for what happened. They could have a daughter who looks like Teresa." Dad sounded as pleased as if he had solved a tricky math problem. "They got her to pretend to be Teresa's ghost."

I looked at my father and almost pitied him—reasonable Dad, the man who depended on logic and common sense. There was no room in his world for the supernatural. No matter how much proof I gave him, he'd never believe me.

"Please," Mom said. "Let's leave, right now, before—"

"Before what?" Dulcie watched us from the shadowy hall. "Before Teresa drags us into the lake and drowns us? Is that what you're scared of?"

Mom got to her feet and faced Dulcie, her fists clenched as if she wanted to punch her sister. "I won't stay here another second!"

Dad put his arm around her. "Claire," he said softly, "it's after ten. We'd never find a room at this hour. And, as much as I love you, I'm not going to sleep in the car."

"Pete's right," Dulcie said. "There aren't many motels, and you can bet they're all filled by now. Why don't I make up the sofa bed?"

Dad yawned. "One night, Claire. We'll go home tomorrow."

Mom turned to Dad, suddenly tearful. "I want to leave, but

168

I'm so tired, I ache all over." Her eyes strayed to the window and the darkness pressing against it.

"How about a glass of warm milk with honey?" Dad asked. "That always helps you relax."

"Can we keep the light on all night?" Mom asked.

Dulcie laughed. "You sound just like Emma."

I braced myself for another quarrel, but before Mom could object, Dulcie added, "I might keep my light on, too."

After I kissed Mom and Dad good night, I gave Dulcie an extra-big hug for admitting she was scared. Maybe there was hope for her and Mom after all.

I climbed the stairs wearily, hoping to fall into bed and sleep till noon, but I should have known better. As usual, Sissy was waiting for me.

21

I saw you bury that bird today," Sissy said. "It had a nice funeral. You sang a song and said the right words. All that fuss for a bird."

"Emma saw a cat kill it. She wanted to——"

"A bird shouldn't get better treatment than a person," Sissy said. "Or am I wrong about that?"

"I know what you're thinking," I said, "but you have a memorial in the cemetery. There must have been a funeral and flowers and the right words and lots of people crying."

"But I'm not buried there, am I?" She held Edith a little tighter. "So none of it counts."

"But nobody knows where you are. Ms. Trent told me people searched the lake, the police sent down divers, they did all they could to find you, but——"

"They didn't try hard enough," Sissy interrupted. "Or I'd be buried in the cemetery instead of——" She broke off with a shudder and went to the window. "Do you think I like being out there?"

I joined her at the window and peered at the lake, barely visible in the rain and darkness. "If you tell me where you are, the police could get you."

"I tried to show you," Sissy said, "but you were scared to come and look. Remember?"

"I thought you were going to push me off the cliff."

Sissy laughed. "I just wanted to show you where I am. Deep down in the cold dark water, under three big rocks. All alone except for Edith . . . and the fish."

"That's where you are?" My voice dropped to a whisper, and my skin prickled with goose bumps. It was almost as if I'd just realized I was actually talking to a girl who'd been dead longer than I'd been alive.

"Why would I lie about it?" Sissy shoved her angry face close to mine. "I'm sick of being there. I want to be buried in the grave-yard where the angel is. Is that too much to ask?"

I drew away from the stale smell of the lake that clung to her. "Of course it's not too much," I stammered. "You *should* be there, it's where you belong."

"If the truth is told and I'm buried properly, if the right words are said over me and people bring flowers and someone cries, then I won't trouble anyone again."

Although it scared me to touch her, I put my arm around her shoulders. She felt solid but cold through and through, and I wished I could warm her somehow.

"Kathie Trent's gotten so old," Sissy said sadly. "Dulcie and Claire, too. I guess Linda must look different. But not me. I'm just the same. I'll never grow up. Or get old."

The sorrow in her voice hurt me. If only I could make it up to her, give her the life she should have had. But there was no way to undo what had happened that day on the lake. Thirty years ago, Sissy had lost her life, her future, and everything that might have been hers.

"Do you think I would've been as pretty as Linda?" Sissy asked. "Would I have gotten married like her, would I have had kids?"

It was hard to answer without crying. "I bet you would have been even prettier than Linda," I told her. "And you would've gotten married and had kids, and all that stuff."

Sissy pulled away, suddenly angry. "Don't you dare feel sorry for me! Just make sure all the things I said should happen *do* happen."

Leaving her words hanging in the air, she vanished, and I was alone at the window. The rain fell softly, the wind blew in the pines, the lake murmured—gloomy sounds, all of them. Sissy was right. What happened to her wasn't fair. It was sad and awful and it hurt my heart.

The next morning, I tiptoed through the living room. Dad snored on the sofa bed, and Mom slept beside him, curled close. Dulcie was in the kitchen, drinking coffee and staring at nothing.

I poured myself a glass of orange juice and sat down across from her. "Telling what happened isn't enough," I whispered. "She wants a proper burial."

Dulcie stared at me over the rim of her mug. "How can we do that? Her body was never found."

"She told me where it is."

Dulcie closed her eyes for a moment. Taking a deep breath, she said, "How will you explain that to the police? A ghost told you? I can imagine their reaction."

"I'll say I had a dream, I'm psychic, I'm—"

"Will this nightmare never end?" Dulcie lowered her head.

I leaned across the table to make my aunt look at me. "Sissy *must* be buried. The right words must be spoken. There must be flowers and somebody crying. She saw us do that for the bird. Doesn't she deserve the same thing?"

"Are you talking about Teresa?" Mom stood in the doorway behind me, her hair tangled from sleep.

Dulcie sighed. "Apparently, Teresa told Ali where her body is. She's demanding a proper burial."

I twisted around in my chair to face Mom. "She just wants peace, Mom. Is that too much to ask?"

"I dreamt about Teresa last night." Mom stood beside me and stroked my hair back from my face, her touch soft and tender, her voice calm. "She begged me to help her pass from this world to the next."

Dulcie jumped up and began pacing around the kitchen. If she'd been a tiger, her tail would have lashed furiously. "She came to me, too," she muttered. "With the same request. Usually, I don't put stock in that sort of nonsense—dreams, ghosts, things left undone, but . . ." She shrugged, and her shoulder blades shifted under her thin T-shirt. "Well, no matter. I agree that Teresa needs to be laid to rest, but how do we explain knowing where her body is? People will think we've known all along."

Dulcie's voice rose as she spoke. "Someone will say I shoved Teresa out of the canoe and left her to drown. Next thing you know, I'll be hauled off to jail."

"I was there, too," Mom said. "What we did was stupid, wrong, horrible, but you didn't push Teresa into the lake. You didn't mean for her to drown."

Dulcie sat back down and rested her head in her hands.

"Do you want more coffee?" I asked.

She surprised me by shaking her head. "All I want is to go to sleep and wake up and find out I dreamt the whole thing. It's what I've wished for all my life—it was a dream, it didn't really happen. But I just go on dreaming. I never wake up."

"I'll tell the reporter Teresa told me where her body is," I said. "I'll say I saw her ghost."

"Maybe—" Dulcie began, but she was interrupted by the arrival of a beat-up red sedan. A short man draped with cameras opened the car door and headed toward the cottage. He wore his gray hair in a scraggly ponytail, his jeans drooped below his belly, and his black T-shirt had an old rock star's picture on it. Mick Jagger, I thought. Or was it one of the Beatles—John, maybe?

"The photographer," Dulcie muttered. "He's early."

Mom ran to wake Dad, Dulcie hurried to greet the photographer, and Emma slid into a chair across the table from me. "Did you see Sissy last night?" she asked me.

"She came to my room."

"She came to my room, too." Emma paused and picked at a scab on her knee. In a low voice, she said, "She told me where her bones are."

"She told me the same thing."

Emma went on picking at the scab. Sunlight slanted through the window behind her and backlit her hair. "She wants to be buried. Like the bird."

"I know." Outside I saw the photographer taking pictures of the cottage. He posed Dulcie, tall and thin in a pair of paint-spattered denim overalls, head tilted, hair curling out of its top-knot. She didn't smile. Her face was serious, contemplative, as if she were acting the part of the repentant adult.

Emma raised her head and looked at me. "If Sissy gets buried, will we ever see her again?"

I reached across the table and patted her hand. "Sissy's here because she wasn't buried. When everything's done properly and people know what happened, she'll be at rest."

"That's what I think, too." Emma sighed and returned her attention to the scab. "I'll miss her, though. Will you?"

"Think of it this way," I said slowly. "Sissy doesn't belong here anymore. Wherever she goes next, she'll be better off. Happier."

"How do you know?" Emma looked at me mournfully. "Maybe she'll just be gone."

Dulcie saved me from trying to answer an impossible question by coming through the kitchen door with the photographer in tow.

"This is Dan Nelson," she said, "from *The Sentinel*. He's come to take a few pictures of you two, as well as some of Claire and me."

Emma looked at him. "I wish you could take a picture of Sissy. She'd like to be in the newspaper."

Mr. Nelson smiled at Emma. "I'm sure I can fit another child into my shots. Is she a friend of yours?"

"Yes," Emma said. "Me and Ali both know her."

Behind Emma's back, Dulcie shook her head at Mr. Nelson, trying to tell him to drop the subject.

"I don't think you can take pictures of ghosts," Emma said.

Ignoring Dulcie, Mr. Nelson squatted down beside Emma and looked her in the eye. "Are you telling me your friend is a ghost?"

He said it in a joking, aren't-you-a-funny-little-thing sort of way, but Emma didn't notice. "Sissy has to be buried in the graveyard, all proper with a funeral and flowers and people crying. Somebody has to get her bones. Ali and me can show you where they are."

"That's enough, sweetie." Dulcie reached for Emma's hand, glanced at me, and then turned to Mr. Nelson. "My niece had a dream about Teresa. She told Ali where her body is."

The photographer looked from Emma to me and then to

Dulcie, his whole face a question mark. "What are you talking about? Nobody knows where Teresa Abbott's body is."

"I believe in psychic powers," Dulcie lied. "If Ali says she knows where the body is, it will be there."

"We didn't just dream Sissy," Emma said. "We *saw* her. We talked to her, we played with her all summer. She was just as real as you!"

Mr. Nelson reacted the way Dad had. "You couldn't have seen her." He glanced at me. "And neither could you."

He had the look of a man who'd seen through many a hoax— UFO's, apparitions, mysterious lights—something that went with a news photographer's job, I supposed.

Mom came to the kitchen door, dressed neatly as usual, the perfect contrast to Dulcie. "You don't believe in ghosts?" she asked Mr. Nelson.

"Of course not."

Dad followed Mom into the kitchen. "I'm afraid you and I are outnumbered," he told Mr. Nelson. "Reason and common sense will not be found in this cottage."

Mr. Nelson made the mistake of laughing. "Maybe it's a female thing."

Dulcie turned on him fiercely. "Gender has nothing to do with this. It's not a hoax, either. Instead of laughing it off, maybe you should give the girls a chance to prove they're right."

"You *have* to believe us," Emma put in. "We promised Sissy."

"Please," Mom added, "let the girls show you the place. Send a diver down. It can't hurt to look."

"Think of it this way," Dad said, still joking. "If the kids are right, you'll have a great story, probably the biggest you'll ever stumble on in Webster's Cove."

Mr. Nelson rubbed his jaw. I could almost hear his thoughts:

national news, Pulitzer Prize, TV talk shows, a best-selling book
. . . on the other hand, I could make a fool of myself, become the
butt of jokes, a laughing stock, never live it down. . . .

"You've got a point," he told Dad. Pulling a cell phone out of a
pocket, he said, "I'll call the police."

A moment later, he said "Hello, Neil? This is Dan Nelson from
The Sentinel. I'm at Gull Cottage doing a recap about the girl
who drowned back in the late seventies."

A slight pause.

"Yes, Teresa Abbott," he went on. "The kids here say they
know where her body is."

Another pause, a little longer this time.

"I'm not sure how they know, but I think it's worth following
up. Maybe you could send a diver."

A pause again.

Mr. Nelson spoke a little louder. "What have you got to lose?"

When he hung up, his face was somewhere between pleased
and worried. "They're sending a diver. He should be here in a
half-hour or so."

Next he called the paper and asked for Ed Jones, the reporter
who'd interviewed Dulcie. "Got something here you might be
interested in," he said.

I could hear Ed Jones's voice but not what he was saying.

"I'll tell you this much," Mr. Nelson went on. "It involves the
Abbott girl's remains—and a hint of the supernatural."

"I'll be right there," Mr. Jones shouted into the phone.

"The supernatural is Ed's thing," Mr. Nelson grinned at Dad
as if to suggest they were linked by common sense and logic. "I
keep telling him he should get a job with one of the rags—*The
National Enquirer,* maybe."

While we waited for the police and Mr. Jones to show up, Mr.

Nelson photographed us in a number of poses, both inside and outside. He even included a few shots of Dad looking skeptical.

When Dulcie showed him the photo of herself, Mom, and Teresa, he borrowed it to make a copy.

Mom grimaced at the sight of it. "You should have destroyed that, Dulcie. Or at least removed Teresa."

Dulcie shrugged. "History's history. You can't change it by destroying a snapshot."

Turning away, she busied herself making a fresh pot of coffee. "There ought to be a pound cake in the pantry," she told me. "Why don't you get that out and fix some blueberries to go with it? I picked a quart yesterday."

By the time the policeman arrived, followed closely by Mr. Jones, we'd all fortified ourselves with cake and blueberries, coffee for the adults, and lemonade for Emma and me.

When she saw the officer at the back door, Dulcie grabbed Mom's hand. For a moment, they looked like little girls clinging to each other, scared and anxious. Neither spoke. They just stood there, holding hands, waiting for what would happen next.

Before the policeman had a chance to introduce himself, a black sedan braked to a sharp stop, and a woman I'd never seen jumped out.

"It's Linda," Mom whispered. Dulcie held her hand tighter.

Sissy's sister came into the kitchen like a blast of wind. Her curves had rounded out, but her hair was still blond, and she wore plenty of lipstick. "You never fooled me," she cried. "I knew all along you were in that canoe with Sissy."

Mom began to apologize, but Dulcie broke in before she finished. "It was an accident," she said. "We never meant to harm Sissy. We were just kids, we—"

"Sissy was just a kid, too!" Linda looked at me. "Younger than her! Why didn't you tell the truth? Do you know how much grief you've caused us? Rich summer people coming here, acting like you're above the law. Well, you should be arrested. You should pay for what you did to my sister!"

The policeman took Linda's arm and gave it a gentle squeeze. "Now, now, Linda, that's enough. I told you not to come out here. I'm not planning to make any arrests. Or press charges. I just want to get some things straight."

Somehow, he managed to calm Linda down. Then he turned to Mom and Dulcie and introduced himself. "I'm Captain Wahl," he said. "I understand you have some new information about Teresa Abbott's remains. The diver's coming by boat, but I thought we could have a little chat before he starts looking."

I wanted to hear what Mom and Dulcie and Linda had to say, but Captain Wahl told Dad to take Emma and me outside. "I'll talk to the girls later."

A motorboat was already tied up at the dock. A man in a wetsuit stood with his back to us, gazing out at the lake. It was one of those rare sunny days, and the water had never looked bluer.

Emma clung to Dad's hand. "Is he going to find Sissy?"

Dad squeezed her hand, his face skeptical. "Maybe."

I grabbed Dad's other hand and held it tight, glad for its familiar shape and warmth. "Yes," I told Emma. "He is."

A few minutes later, Captain Wahl joined us. The others trailed behind, Mom and Dulcie close together, Linda a few steps back, clearly separating herself from them. The reporter and photographer brought up the rear, heads together, exchanging opinions.

Captain Wahl took Emma and me aside. "Tell me again how you know where the body is."

"It's just bones now," Emma whispered.

"Yes, right." Captain Wahl nodded and wrote something in a little notebook. "But how do you know where the bones are?"

"Sissy told us."

"Sissy's Teresa's ghost," I added. "Emma and I have seen her lots of times. Honest we have. Last night she told us both where her . . . where she is." I couldn't bring myself to refer to Sissy's bones or her skeleton.

"A ghost." He nodded and made a few more notes. I knew he didn't believe us, but he played along as if he did. "Will you show me where you think the bones are?"

Emma and I set out along the path. Captain Wahl called down to the diver to follow in his boat. With Linda on our heels and the others close behind her, we made our way to the high point Sissy had taken me to. More fearless than I, Emma walked to the edge and pointed down.

"See those three big rocks? That's where the bones are."

Captain Wahl peered down at the calm water. "You're sure, honey?"

"Sissy told me. And she told Ali, too."

I nodded. "This is the place."

Captain Wahl signaled, and the diver anchored his boat and slipped into the water. He was gone a long time.

"Did he drown?" Emma asked.

"He has an oxygen tank," I told her. "So he can breathe under water."

At last the diver came to the surface. "I don't know how the girls knew," he called up to the captain, "but the bones are there."

Linda began to cry. "If only Mom and Dad were still alive, if only they knew she's been found."

Dulcie and Mom cried, too, but Dad stood there like a man in shock. The photographer looked stunned as well. His and Dad's concept of the world had suffered a serious blow. In contrast, the reporter grinned broadly.

Captain Wahl was the only one to speak. "Incredible," he said.

Emma took my hand and pointed. "Look," she whispered.

In the shadows under the pines, Sissy gave a thumbs-up and vanished before anyone else saw her.

Dad reached out for Emma and me. "Let's go back to the cottage."

~∽22∽~

The rest of the day dragged slowly past. Emma spent most of it sleeping, exhausted, I guess, by all that had happened. The policeman left, still puzzled. With a few more nasty comments, Linda departed. The photographer and Dad sat on the deck trying to find other explanations for the discovery of Teresa Abbott's remains. The reporter sat near them, still grinning, and typing away on his laptop. In the end, all three were left with the possibility that Emma and I had truly seen a ghost.

Live Action News showed up in the afternoon, along with most of the population of Webster's Cove. Tourists tramped through the yard and followed the trail to the cliff top, snapping pictures of everything with their little cameras. We were interviewed all over again by the TV reporter and videotaped by their photographers.

The media people insisted on waking Emma so they could talk to both of the girls who saw the ghost. Tired and cranky, Emma clung to Dulcie and cried. I overheard the reporter say in a hushed tone, "Four-year-old Emma, clearly traumatized by her encounter with the supernatural, sobs in her mother's arms."

Fed up, I sneaked away into the woods. Safe from reporters and tourists, I sat down and leaned against a tree trunk. "They all know now, Sissy," I said to myself. "Everyone in the state of Maine and probably the rest of the country, too."

Sissy stepped out from behind the tree, cradling Edith in the crook of her arm, her silvery hair bright against the gloomy woods. With a sigh, she sank onto the mossy ground beside me, closed her eyes, and rested her head against the tree.

"Are you okay?" I asked.

Sissy yawned. "Just tired," she murmured. "Really, really tired. All those people running around, asking questions, taking pictures. Even when they can't see you, being famous is hard on a person."

"I couldn't take it anymore, either," I confessed. "That's why I'm hiding in the woods."

"Do you think they'll bury me soon?"

"The day after tomorrow, I heard." Uncomfortable with her question, I toyed with a twig, bending it this way and that, avoiding her eyes. It bothered me to talk about her burial with her sitting beside me, as real as ever.

"That's good." Her sigh was as soft as a breeze in the treetops. "I'm not sure how much longer I can stay."

"Where are you going?" I asked, forgetting for a moment she wasn't an ordinary girl about to leave on a trip.

Sissy grinned. "That's for me to know—and you to find out."

My discomfort returned, and I twisted the twig again. When it broke with a loud snap, I tossed the pieces away.

Sissy held up her arm. "Look, you can almost see through it."

I turned my head. "Don't."

Sissy came closer. "Why? Does it scare you?"

When I slid away from her, she laughed out loud. "Better watch out. I might take you with me."

"Stop it. That's not funny."

Still laughing, she seized my arm. "Don't you like me even a little bit?"

Chilled by the touch of her hand, I pulled away and jumped to my feet, ready to run.

"No," Sissy cried. "Don't go, Ali. I was just teasing."

I hesitated, rubbing my arm to warm the spot she'd grabbed. "How do I know you're not lying?"

With narrowed eyes, Sissy stared at me. "If I wanted to kill you, I'd have drowned you and Emma both when I had the chance. Just sit with me awhile. I'll be gone soon."

Cautiously, I sat down a few feet away from her, scared to get too close.

"All I really wanted was a friend." She poked at the moss with a stick, scratching lines in it. "When Dulcie came along, I thought she was going to be my friend, but then she had to go and throw Edith in the lake and ruin everything. I wish she hadn't done that."

"She wishes she hadn't done it, too."

Sissy nodded wearily. "But she did. And look at all the trouble she caused."

"She didn't think you'd jump in the water."

Sissy gouged the moss savagely, tearing up bits of it and revealing the dark soil it grew from. "Okay, okay, it was a dumb thing to do. Don't you think I know that now?"

"I've done plenty of dumb things," I said. "Everybody has. It's just that—" I broke off and watched a ladybug settle on a leaf beside me.

"It's just that most people don't end up like me," Sissy finished my sentence.

I sighed and nudged the ladybug gently into the air. *Fly away home.*

"The water was deep and dark and cold," Sissy said, "and I

kept sinking down. I tried and tried, but I couldn't swim up to the top."

Suddenly, she reached out and touched my cheek. "You're crying."

"I know."

Sissy watched the tears run down my cheeks. "If things had been different," she said, "if I was like you instead of—well, what I am—do you think we would be friends?"

Once I would have said no without even thinking, but things had changed between Sissy and me. "Yes, I think so."

"Me, too." Sissy smiled and leaned back against the tree. Her eyelids fluttered shut, and she seemed to sleep.

I didn't know whether she wanted me to leave or stay, so I sat beside her and waited for her to wake up. While we'd been talking, the sky had begun clouding over. A gust of wind turned the leaves white-side-up, a sure sign of rain Dad always said.

When Sissy opened her eyes, I got to my feet. "I should go home before it starts raining."

Sissy stayed where she was, her back against the tree, her legs stretched out in front of her. "Bye, Ali."

"Will I see you again?"

"Maybe." She smiled at me, one of her rare real smiles.

I waved and left her there. I didn't look back.

By the time I reached the cottage, rain was coming down hard, and the last of the sightseers were driving away, leaving the driveway rutted and filled with puddles.

A couple of days later, the people in Webster's Cove held a funeral for Sissy, just as I'd told her they would. In the graveyard, over a hundred people huddled under umbrellas and listened to a minister read a tribute to a child long lost but now found. He led a prayer. We cried and threw flowers on the small coffin as it was lowered into the grave at the angel's feet.

Afterward, in the warmth of Gull Cottage, Mom and Dad discussed their plans to drive home the next day.

"Do you want to come with us?" Mom asked me.

Dulcie patted my hand. "I'll understand if you leave," she said. "I've been a witch."

Emma threw her arms around me. "Please stay," she whispered.

I hugged Emma hard. "Okay, okay, I'll stay."

Mom opened her mouth to protest, but Dad shook his head. "Summer's more than half over. Ali will be home before we know it."

So it was settled. My parents went home, and I remained at the lake. Dulcie returned to her studio and her work. She decided the paintings weren't as bad as she'd thought. One night at dinner, she told us she was going to call her show "Deep and Dark and Dangerous, a Study of Water's Changing Moods."

On sunny days, Emma and I swam and built sandcastles. We went to Smoochie's, and I talked Emma into trying something besides chocolate. On rainy days we drew and read and made clay figures. I finished *To Kill a Mockingbird* and began *A Separate Peace.* The summer had taken a turn to the ordinary.

But not quite. Just before Dulcie planned to return to New York, Emma and I decided to visit the graveyard. On the way, we each gathered a handful of wildflowers. Sissy would like them, Emma said.

Despite the sunlight, the graveyard was in shadows. A splash or two of light dappled the stone angel and the new grave at its feet.

Emma seized my hand. "Look," she whispered.

Missing one arm, hair matted and dirty, skin stained, Edith lay on the earth that was heaped over Sissy. Emma ran to the grave, but I hesitated, not sure how to interpret the doll's presence. Had Sissy left her there for Emma? Or did she want Edith to stay where she was?

Something stirred in the shadows behind the angel. In the dim light, I saw Sissy. For the first time she looked like what she was, nearly transparent, too thin to cast a shadow, her voice a whisper. "The doll's for you, Emma. To keep."

Emma reached out as if to embrace Sissy, but her arms closed on nothing. Sissy was gone. Gone for good.

Tearfully, Emma laid her flowers on the grave and picked up the doll. "Sissy wants me to have Edith."

I laid my flowers beside Emma's. Silently, the two of us stood together, thinking our own thoughts of Sissy.

After a long moment, I turned to Emma. "Let's go home," I said softly.

Hand in hand, we left Sissy resting peacefully under the angel's protective hand.